BROTHER OF THE KID

'Mount up, ride, and don't come back!'
That was Marshal Cliff Wood's order, but
Jim Lawson didn't take it lying down.
He'd been forced out of the Redrock
country once; now he was back again—to
stay. He was determined to stick it out,
even though he had to fight the law, the
hostility of the townspeople, and his bitter
enemy, Dave Culpepper. True, Jim's
brother was an outlaw and a killer. But
Jim had rights as a decent citizen. He had
land and cattle, too, that he swore no two-
bit, four-flushing, son-of-a-buzzard was
going to take away from him.

BROTHER OF THE KID

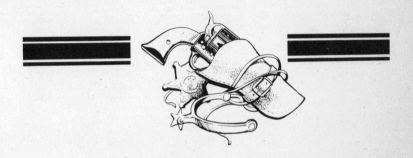

Paul Evan Lehman

ATLANTIC LARGE PRINT
Chivers Press, Bath, England.
John Curley & Associates Inc.,
South Yarmouth, Mass., USA.

Library of Congress Cataloging in Publication Data

Lehman, Paul Evan.   Allen County Public Library
    Brother of the kid.   Ft. Wayne, Indiana

    "Atlantic large print."
      1. Large type books.   I. Title.
    [PS3523.E434B7 1985]   813'.54   84–23897
    ISBN 0–89340–820–4 (lg. print)

British Library Cataloguing in Publication Data

Lehman, Paul Evan
    Brother of the Kid.—Large print ed.—
    (Atlantic large print)
    I. Title
    813'.54[F]   PS3523.E434

    ISBN 0–7451–9105–3

This Large Print edition is published by Chivers Press, England, and
John Curley & Associates, Inc, U.S.A. 1986

Published by arrangement with Donald MacCampbell, Inc

U.K. Hardback ISBN 0 7451 9105 3
U.S.A. Softback ISBN 0 89340 820 4

DEDICATED TO PAULA JEAN

7093210

CONTENTS

CHAPTER ONE

ESCAPE

The Kid was going to escape. He was locked securely in a strong cell, a night-and-day vigilance over him was maintained with hourly visits by a guard, he had no weapon to aid him; nevertheless, he was going to escape. He had planned carefully and waited patiently and now the time had come.

His name was Edward Lawson, but they had not known that when they first called him the Kid. He was the leader of a small band of highwaymen who had made it unprofitable for stage lines to transport gold and had multiplied the gray hairs of railway officials, but the Kid always worked with his features hidden by a mask and there was nothing distinctive in the clothing he wore or the horse he rode. The impression of youth was given by his slimness, his alert bearing, the swift, easy grace of his movements and his audacity. They had called him the Kid and the Kid he remained even after the day when he and three pals held up the Redrock bank and took twenty thousand dollars in cash.

Edward Lawson had left home when he was

1

seventeen with the announced purpose of getting work on a ranch in a neighboring state; now he was twenty-one and in the intervening years he had killed three men. The Kid claimed these killings were justified, necessitated by the stubborn loyalty of a bank teller and the overzealous efforts of two lawmen who would willingly have sacrificed an arm for the honor of capturing or killing him; but the world in general held that the circumstances attending the shootings had been brought about by the criminal actions of the Kid himself, and wholeheartedly condemned him.

The specific killing for which he had been tried and sentenced to hang was that of Arthur Fenton, cashier of the Redrock bank. It had occurred when the Kid was backing his way out of the bank with a sack containing the twenty thousand dollars in one hand and his very efficient Colt in the other. Fenton, bravely but unwisely, snatched a gun from beneath the counter and the Kid shot him squarely between the eyes. The gang had worked with their usual speed, and within three minutes from the time they had entered Redrock they were dashing along the street at a thundering gallop, threatening guns in their hands and still wearing their masks.

But for Sheriff Tom Payne they might have

2

made it without a hitch. The sheriff had his office at Springwater, the county seat, and ordinarily would have been in that town; but on this particular day he had ridden over to see the Redrock marshal on business and was in the latter's office when the four sped past.

It would be more accurate to say that three sped past; the fourth had trouble with his horse and was trailing his companions by ten yards. Half of those ten yards spelled the margin of his undoing; Sheriff Payne, in his brief glimpse of the flying three in front, saw the masks and the guns and knew that the Kid's gang was on the rampage again. He yanked out his Colt, fired through the glass of the window at the one who was trailing, and dropped the bandit's horse. The rider took a hard fall and before he could regain his wits and his feet Payne and the marshal had pounced upon him. To save his own skin he had named the Kid as Fenton's killer and had identified him as Edward Lawson.

The identification came as a shock to Tom Payne, for the Kid's father, John Lawson, owned a small ranch adjoining that of the sheriff and the Paynes and Lawsons had been firm friends for many years. The sheriff had never for a moment associated the young man who had left home to seek his fortune in another state with the notorious Kid. He could not, did not, let the friendship sway him in the performance of his duty; that night he walked into the Lawson house while they were eating supper and arrested the Kid without a struggle. The Kid had not known of his betrayal and was ten feet away from his gun.

Payne took no chances with his prisoner. The Kid was a dangerous man and two of his pals were still free and might attempt a rescue. The Redrock marshal and a couple of deputies formed a bodyguard on the ride to Springwater and the Kid was locked in a cell by himself and put under constant surveillance. In time he was tried for the death of Arthur Fenton, found guilty in a matter of minutes, and sentenced to death by hanging.

He was returned to jail to await the morning of execution, a morning which the Kid had determined would never dawn. He was going to escape.

There would be no outside aid, he knew; the two other members of the gang had fled the state and would not risk coming back. He had not so much as a bit of broken crockery, for every dish and piece of cutlery was counted before and after each meal. There would be no chance of jumping the guard who fetched his meals, for the tray was pushed through a narrow opening at the bottom of the cage and recovered in the same manner. The

4

cell was never entered by a guard unless a second one stood outside with his gun trained on the Kid. There seemed not the remotest chance that Edward Lawson would cheat the noose, but the Kid was sure he had found the way.

Realizing that he would be found guilty and condemned, he had formed his plan during the week which preceded his trial. He complained about the condition of his cell to Ben Turner, one of his guards, and demanded that it be swept out. Ben Turner hated the Kid with a hatred that was almost fanatic. He had reason to hate Ed Lawson, for one of the men the Kid had shot was Ben's brother-in-law. He taunted the Kid unmercifully on every occasion that offered itself, stating that he had obtained the privilege of springing the trap which would send the Kid into eternity and would enjoy watching him dance at the end of the rope. Turner received with scorn the demand that the cell be cleaned.

'Figger you'll get me inside and jump me, huh? You'd sure enough like to do that, and I'm kinda tempted to give you the chance so's I can plug you when you try it. But I want to see you dance, Kid. I sure do. So you got a dirty cell, huh? Well, we can fix that. You can sweep it out yourself.'

So Ben found an old broom and broke the

handle off six inches from the bound straws and slipped it through the wicket. He said, 'There you are. If you're so danged anxious to clean up, git down on your hands and knees and sweep all you want to.'

It was just what the Kid had hoped for, but he hid his elation from Ben. He cursed him dispassionately and, bending over, went to work with the abbreviated broom while Ben watched and jeered. Every day he swept out the cell, cursing Ben for removing the handle. When he was returned to the cell with the sentence of death hanging over him, the broom was still there and he continued to use it. That broom, he determined, was going to sweep him to freedom one day.

It took an astute mind to conceive a plan whereby the broom could serve as the key to freedom. It was not a weapon; the worn straws were about as lethal as a fly-swatter, the handle was so short that it could not be used as a club, and the tough wood could not be sharpened into a stabbing instrument because of the dullness of the knife which came with the Kid's meals. It was just the stub of an old, worn-out broom; no more. So thought Ben Turner and the other guard, Ed Hall. But the Kid knew better.

He was forced to wait until the day before his scheduled execution to put his plan to work, because there was a man in the second cell from him who was not to be released until that time and the Kid dared not risk having the guards tipped off. The only other occupant of the jail was on the other side of the corridor and at the far end of the cell block. He would not be able to follow the Kid's movements while he sat on his bunk eating his supper. And it had to be at suppertime when the lamp hanging from the corridor ceiling left Kid's cell in gloom.

The process of serving supper to the prisoners never varied. At five-thirty one of the guards went to the restaurant and helped the owner carry the utensils and containers of food to the jail office. Here the food was dished out on trays which were carried by the guards into the cell room and thrust, one at a time, through the wickets at the foot of the cages. One guard then went out for his supper.

When he returned, both men collected the emptied trays and checked the dishes and cutlery. The second guard carried them back to the restaurant when he went out for his supper. The Kid had been a tenant of the jail long enough to know the whole procedure.

On this night, it was Ed Hall who pushed the tray through the wicket and said, 'Come and get it, Kid.'

7

Ben Turner, hand on gun butt, glared banefully through the bars and said, 'And eat hearty. You ain't gonna get no breakfast. No use fillin' your belly just before stretchin' your neck.'

The Kid gave him a long look. 'You'll never see me hang, Ben.'

'The hell I won't! I'm gonna spring the trap. I'm gonna spring it from below, where I can get a good look at you dancin'.'

Ed Hall protested. 'Aw, what's the use of rubbin' it in, Ben? Let him alone.' He went along the corridor with the tray for their remaining prisoner and Ben stood outside the Kid's cell watching him eat.

If he had expected to find the Kid without an appetite he was disappointed. Ed Lawson carried the tray back to his bunk, sat down with it beside him and went to work hungrily, ignoring the watching man. Hall came back empty-handed and said gruffly, 'Come on, Ben; your turn to eat first.'

Ben grunted and followed Hall into the office.

The Kid ate leisurely, using his mental clock to time himself. He heard the opening and closing of the outside door which told of Ben's departure, heard the scrape of a chair as Hall settled himself at the desk. Then came the rustle of the paper that Ed was reading.

The Kid finished, placed the tray on the floor by the bunk, took up the dull knife and went to the corner where his stub of broom stood. With the knife he removed the brad which secured the end of the thin wire holding the straws to the handle. This out, he proceeded to unwind the wire. Four feet of thin wire was going to get him through iron bars an inch thick and walls of solid stone.

He made a small loop at one end, winding the wire tightly so that it would not pull out; through this loop he ran the free end, forming a noose wide enough to pass over his head. He grinned at the thought that he had just fashioned a duplicate of the one which Ben Turner was gloatingly anticipating passing over his head the following morning.

He walked to the front of the cell, listened for the rustle of paper which told him Ed Hall was still at the desk, then got on the bunk at the back of the cell. He could just reach the bars which formed the top of the cage in which he was imprisoned. He ran the free end of the wire over one of them and secured it by winding the slack around the dangling part. He tested it briefly, putting his weight on it.

He got down from the bunk and took the newspaper which Hall had given him to read and folded it half a dozen times to form a thick long pad some three inches wide. He wrapped

9

this carefully about his neck, then turned up his coat collar so that it was entirely covered. He got back on the bunk, took off his hat, slipped his head through the noose with the honda of the loop at the back, drew it tight so that the pressure was on coat collar and the pad beneath, then put on his hat and stood on the edge of the bunk waiting.

He heard the front door open and close, heard Ben Turner say, 'All right; we can pick up the stuff and you can get goin'.' He heard the scrape of the chair as Hall got to his feet.

The Kid lowered himself several inches, felt the noose tighten about his neck, then removed one foot from the bunk, swung lightly outward, removed the other. The wire loop tightened about his neck nearly strangling him, but the cloth and paper prevented its cutting into his flesh. He let his body go limp, arms and legs dangling lifelessly; his head sagged downward, the hatbrim hiding his face. He kept his eyes open in a dead stare.

He saw them come out of the office, Hall in the lead. He saw Hall glance down at the wicket where his tray should have been, then look swiftly into the gloomy cell. Hall gave a startled cry. 'Good gosh, Ben! Look!'

Ben looked and cried, 'Hanged himself with that broom wire! Why, the double-crossin'

10

skunk!' He swore harshly and his hand flashed to the key ring at his belt. 'The low-down yella-belly! Get them wire cutters outa the office, Ed. And make it fast.'

Hall ran for the office and Ben thrust a key into the lock. He was cursing the Kid and muttering things about cowardice and cheating the law and robbing him of his anticipated pleasure. He ran across the floor to the hanging Kid, took a lax hand and felt of it. He yelled, 'Hurry up, Ed! He's still warm!'

Ed came at the run, wire cutters in hand. Ben snapped, 'Up on the bunk and cut him loose. I'll catch him when he falls.' He circled the Kid's legs and the body dropped.

The Kid let his weight sag forward and Ben staggered back, trying to regain his balance. He recovered and let the body slip downward so that it would have the support of the floor beneath it. The Kid's hands, still at his side, slid down Turner's body and the left one brushed the butt of Turner's Colt. The corpse came to life.

The Kid, feet now on the ground, pushed Turner backwards with his right hand and yanked out the Colt with his left. He wasted no movement, lost not a second; the left hand arced around and the sixgun roared and Ben staggered back and fell, shot through the stomach. His glaring eyes reflected surprise

11

and pain and an awful comprehension. He gasped, 'Foxed me, by Gawd!'

The Kid wheeled and the Colt leveled once more. Ed Hall stood petrified on the bunk. He had no time to get out his gun. The Kid said, 'Do just as I tell you, Ed, and I won't hurt you. Get your hands up.'

Hall obeyed instantly, the fear of death on his face. The Kid reached out and unbuckled Hall's gun belt and caught it as it fell. He backed away and buckled it about him. Turner was groaning in agony.

The Kid said, 'Lay down on the bunk, Ed,' and Hall obeyed.

The Kid searched him, taking what money Hall had and a pair of handcuffs. He put the money into his pocket, then cuffed Hall to the iron bunk. 'You start yellin',' he said ominously, 'and I'll come back and kill you.'

He turned and knelt beside Ben. He cursed the dying man. 'Told you you'd never see me hang, you louse. You been askin' for this for a long time; that's why I shot you through the guts. You'll die, but you'll get a taste of hell before you ever reach it.'

He searched the groaning man roughly, taking what money he had in his pockets, then got up, backed out of the cell and locked the door after him. He went swiftly along the corridor. The prisoner in the last cell was

12

gripping the bars and staring at him. The Kid said, 'Want out?' and the fellow shook his head dumbly.

The Kid opened the back door, went out swiftly and closed it behind him. He took the folded paper from around his neck and dropped it, then crossed the alley and went into the stable. A lighted lantern hung from a beam. He put Turner's rig on Turner's horse, figuring that Ben wouldn't need either on his trip to the Great Beyond. He mounted and rode around the stable and out on the range. He put the horse to a brisk canter, heading for the near-by hills. When he had entered them he reined down to a walk.

Presently he began to hum a tune. He wasn't going to hang on the morrow and he had settled his score with Ben Turner. The Kid felt good.

CHAPTER TWO

PERSECUTION

Revelation that the notorious Kid was in reality Edward Lawson had been a shock to his father, his mother and his seventeen-year-old brother. John Lawson aged twenty years

13

in the four months following his son's capture; Nellie Lawson lost her cheerful buoyancy and no longer sang as she went about her work; young Jimmie became somber and brooding under the gibes of other boys. At first, bitterly resenting the taunts which were flung at him, Jimmie fought his tormentors singly or in groups; reluctant realization of the full extent of Ed's guilt brought with it a sullen resignation beneath which his resentment was smothered. One can fight to the death for a cause in which one believes, but in Ed's case the evidence against him was so strong that even such a loyal brother as Jimmie could find no excuse for defending him. So he smoldered and endured.

It was four o'clock of a Saturday afternoon when Jimmie Lawson, unaware of his brother's escape, drove the buckboard into Redrock for the week's supplies. The town was quiescent; after the supper hour it would fill up and things would begin to hum. Miners would come in from the hills and creeks and cowboys from scattered ranches would gallop up and down the wide, crooked street whooping it up as was their wont on Saturday nights. Jimmie had driven in early to avoid the rush.

Quiet as it was, Jimmie made his way along the street through an atmosphere of hostility.

The store at which the Lawsons were forced to trade had been robbed on two occasions by the Kid and his gang, Redrock had been made twenty thousand dollars the poorer by the bank robbery, and Art Fenton, a well-liked local man, had been wantonly shot by the Kid. Consequently Redrock resented the Lawsons and did not hesitate to show its resentment.

Young Jim tied his team outside Jeb Culpepper's general store and started up the steps. Jeb's son Dave was sweeping some trash through the doorway; he stopped and glared down at Jim.

'You can't come in,' he said. 'Rein around and beat it.'

Dave Culpepper was two years older than Jimmie, with sleek dark hair which he plastered carefully on both sides of a straight white part, dark eyes which could flash or smolder, and a budding mustache which he nursed and pampered as a stamp of his masculinity. The girls thought him handsome.

Jimmie halted. 'Why can't I come in?'

'Because you can't. We're not selling to the kin of a killer.'

A wave of hot resentment flooded over Jim and touched his smooth cheeks with pink. Dave Culpepper had been his chief tormentor

15

and he had suffered two trouncings at the hands of the older, heavier boy. He set himself to take another one.

'Pop sent me in for supplies and this is the only store where I can get them. I'm paying cash and you got no right to refuse me.'

He took another upward step, and Dave gave a quick flip with the broom which sent the trash flying into Jim's face. The dirt blinded him momentarily, and Jimmie halted to rub the dust from his eyes. The tears started flowing and through them he could see the contorted face of Dave Culpepper. Dave was speaking swiftly, viciously.

'I said you ain't coming in! The old man said so too. We don't want your trade. We kind of pitied you before today, figuring that you had to eat no matter what that killer brother of yours had done; but after today there ain't no more sympathy for the Lawsons. Now beat it.'

Jim didn't know how the day's events had altered the situation and didn't stop to inquire. He was filled with a sudden hot rage that hurled him upward towards the belligerent Dave Culpepper. He was met in mid-air by the brush end of the broom which caught him in the chest and flung him backwards. Instinctively he grasped at it and caught it, and as he fell he gave it the hardest yank of which he was capable. Dave gripping the broom, was pulled off his feet; he came hurtling down the steps after Jim, went clear over him and landed sprawling on the plank sidewalk.

The fall temporarily stunned him and Jimmie was quick to take advantage; he came to his feet with the quickness of a cougar and hurled himself atop Dave. All the pent-up resentment and hatred within him flowed into his fists; he hammered the older boy unmercifully, punishing him with every blow. Dave squirmed and dodged and twisted and tried to strike back, but his superior weight was of no use to him now.

'You take that back!' Jim was saying between tight lips. 'Take back every word or I'll kill you!'

Somebody leaped on his back and put their arms about his throat. He raised his hands to grip the encircling arms and tear at them, but another boy came running across the street and struck him in the face. Still another joined the struggling, heaving group, and Jimmie felt the sharp pain of a kick in his ribs. They had ganged up on him.

He fought savagely but hopelessly. Dave squirmed out from under him and their combined weight flattened Jimmie on the sidewalk. His mind was going blank when he

17

suddenly realized that a sharp voice was ordering them to quit and that the weight upon him was gone. He pushed himself to hands and knees and a strong hand gripped his arm and pulled him to his feet.

Sheriff Tom Payne said, 'Now what's this all about?'

Panting and gasping for breath, Jim told him. 'Dave won't let me in the store. He swept dirt in my eyes and tried to push me off the steps with a broom. I yanked him down and I was goin' to kill him.'

'I don't think you were, Jimmie; though I ain't sayin' you didn't have cause.' He released Jimmie and turned to the sullen group of boys. 'You kids get on about your business. Go on!' They shuffled away, slowly, resentfully, and the sheriff spoke to Dave. 'Why wouldn't you let him in the store?'

'You know why,' said Dave hotly. 'You know what his brother Ed done. Dad said the Lawsons were finished in our store.'

'He did, huh? We'll see about that. Come on in, Jim.'

He strode up the steps and Jimmie followed him. He was sore, his face was cut, and his side ached where he had been kicked; but he tried to walk without showing how badly he had been hurt. He got out his handkerchief and wiped off his face as they went

18

into the store.

Jeb Culpepper was standing just within the doorway, his eyes glinting as they rested on Jim.

Sheriff Payne said, 'Jimmie has an order for some stuff. Fill it.'

Jeb Culpepper clamped his jaws together and shook his head. 'No. I said the Lawsons couldn't get any more goods here, and that stands.'

'They owe you any money?'

'No; but—'

'Runnin' a public store, ain't you?'

'Yes; but—'

'Then give him what he wants or I'll advise his father to sue you for damages. And I'm tellin' you here and now that he'll win his suit.'

Money was Jeb Culpepper's god; the assurance of the sheriff that he would most certainly part with some of it if he didn't fulfill the order hit him where it hurt.

'But you know what happened yesterday,' he protested. 'In my opinion the whole Lawson family oughta be run out of Redrock.'

'Your opinion don't run one, two, three with that of a judge. Now shut up and fill the boy's order. I'll stick around and see that you do it proper. No short weight, Jeb. Against the law, you know.'

19

Culpepper took the list from Jim and went behind the counter and started jerking articles from the shelves as though each one of them had offered him a personal affront. Jim stood white-faced and tight-lipped, waiting.

Payne said mildly, 'How's things on the Lazy L, Jimmie? You and that tomboy gal of mine still chasin' the black stallion?'

The tautness left Jim's face. Sheriff Payne was like a second father to him. Payne's ranch, adjacent to the Lazy L, was managed by his brother while its owner performed his duties as sheriff, and Payne's fourteen-year-old daughter, Nancy, was Jimmie's pal. The black stallion led a small bunch of wild horses that roamed the mesa, and in their youthful determination to trap and tame him Jimmie and Nancy had ridden their ponies into the ground on many a fruitless chase.

Jim smiled faintly. 'We're still chasin' him. He's sure some horse.'

'Too much horse for you youngsters, I reckon.'

They started talking horses then, and continued to talk them until Jeb had put up the order. When he had it packed in a box, Jimmie paid him and started for the buckboard with his load.

Payne said, 'I'll ride out with you. I want to see your father.'

20

They made it to the Lazy L in an hour and found John Lawson splitting wood. Jimmie drove to the house and unloaded his supplies, then unhitched and put up the horses, fed them and pushed the buckboard under the shed. Sheriff Payne had dismounted by the wood pile, had spoken briefly with John Lawson and then had gone with him into the house. He came out as Jimmie finished, mounted his horse and rode away.

John Lawson came out a moment later and Jimmie saw that his shoulders sagged and that he walked slouchingly and with bowed head. He went around the wood pile and sat down heavily on the saw buck.

Jim went over to him and said, 'What's wrong, Pop?'

Lawson raised a face contorted with grief. His eyes were dull.

'Your brother Ed. He escaped from the courthouse last night.'

Jimmie felt a little surge of elation. 'Then they won't hang him!'

'Yes, they'll hang him in the end. Unless they shoot him first. I hope to God they do! It's a hard thing for a father to say of his own son, but I hope they do. It'll be over then, and clean.'

'But, Pop! You can't wish anything like that! Ed's your son; your own flesh and blood.'

21

'Ed's a killer. Four times over. He shot Ben Turner makin' his getaway. And he didn't shoot him clean; he made him suffer by shootin' him through the stomach. Ben's still alive but there's no chance for him.'

Jim was shocked but still loyal. 'Ben had it comin'. He's been tauntin' Ed about hangin'. He had no right to do that.'

John Lawson said wearily, 'There's no excuse for torturin' a man. If Ed had to shoot him he might have made a clean job of it like he would with a hurt animal. He had no right to torture Ben.'

'Does—does Mom know?'

'Not that he killed Ben. She knows he escaped; Tom had to have an excuse for searchin' the house so he told her. But she don't know that he's killed another. She'll find it out sooner or later: Redrock'll take care of that.'

He got up and stood tensely for a moment, his eyes on the distant horizon. 'We can't stay here, Jim. The whole town'll be down on us now. Tom told me about Jeb Culpepper not wantin' to fill our order. They'll bedevil us until they break us; they'll do their best to make you follow in Ed's footsteps. And your mother, it'll kill her. Nobody to visit with, nobody who'll even speak to us on the street. She ain't been the same since Ed's trial.

You and me can take it, but it'll kill her sure.'

Jimmie looked slowly about him, taking in the familiar scenes he had known ever since his birth, and this time he couldn't swallow the lump that rose in his throat.

'You mean—leave Redrock? Leave the Lazy L?'

'Yes. Just as soon as I can locate some good range. There's no use stayin' now.' The rigidity went out of his frame and once more his shoulders drooped. He said in a dull voice, 'Supper's about ready,' and shuffled away towards the house.

Supper was a dull affair. Nobody was hungry. Mrs. Lawson's eyes were red and Jimmie knew she had been crying. He excused himself and went outside to do the evening chores. It was still light when he had finished, and as he looked out across the rolling range he saw a rider who was coming hell bent and knew it for Nancy Payne.

Some of the somberness left him, for he was still a boy and sight of his pal gave a lift to his spirit. He hurried to meet her as she slipped from her saddle. Her cheeks were flushed and her eyes sparkled with excitement.

She cried, 'Know what, Jimmie? The black stallion's back on the mesa!'

'You sure?'

'I saw him. And he saw me, too. I rode up the side and there he was. He just stood there and looked at me with his mane flying in the wind, and he actually winked at me!'

'Aw-w-w!'

'Well, it looked like he did. I believe he likes us to chase him. But we'll get him the next time. I've figured out a way to catch him.'

'How?'

Jim was skeptical. He looked at the high, flat-topped mesa which rose within a mile of the Lazy L. There were two ways of reaching its top. On the south side a narrow fissure split it from the top to base, forming a canyon whose bed sloped upward to its top. One could follow this. On the west side a trail snaked up the almost perpendicular wall. It was not more than three feet wide at any point and the footing was treacherous; but these two had ascended and descended it so often that they could have negotiated it blindfolded.

The black stallion and his band used both paths, which was why he had not been caught by the two youthful horse hunters. If they chased him up one trail, he went down the other; if Nancy took the cliff and Jimmie the canyon they had the satisfaction of trapping the black stallion on the top of the mesa but no means of running him down; for as sure as one

24

of them left his post to do the chasing, the stallion promptly ducked down the path which had been left open. As Nancy put it in bitter exasperation, one of them should have been twins.

So Jimmie was skeptical; but this time Nancy really had something.

She slid to the ground and sat cross-legged, and Jim hunkered down on his heels facing her. She said, 'Lookit! You know how narrow that canyon trail is at the bottom; well, if we block it we can go up the cliff path and chase him down into the canyon. When he reaches the bottom he can't get out and we'll be right behind him. We got him.'

'Yeah? How do you figure on blockin' this end?'

'We'll cut poles and build a barrier. It's not more'n ten feet wide.'

'How'll we make 'em stick? You can't dig postholes in rock and you can't drive nails either.'

Nancy made an impatient gesture. 'We'll make something like a corral gate and prop it up and brace it and pile rocks behind it.'

Jim thought this over. 'Might do. But it'll take a lot of work.'

'Who cares? Tomorrow's Sunday; we got all day.'

'Well, we can try it. You meet me there

after I got the chores done.'

'I'll be there.' She got nimbly to her feet. 'I got to be getting back. Dad told me to be sure to be home before dark.' She swung up on her pony and settled herself in the saddle, then looked down at him, her small face grave.

'I hear Ed got away.'

'Yeah.' Some of the misery which had left him returned.

'You mustn't let it get you down, Jimmie.'

'Who is?'

'You are. You act like it was you that did all the robbing and shooting. It isn't. Ed's being an outlaw doesn't make you one.'

'That's what you think,' said Jimmy bitterly. 'Folks treat us like we were poison. They used to stop on the street and talk and joke; now they cross to the other side to keep from meetin' us.'

'Not all of them. I don't. Dad don't. Those that do are the ones that just pretended to be your friends. They'd talk about you behind your back the first chance they got. *I'll* stop and talk to you anywhere, any time. So'll Dad.'

Jimmie choked up and couldn't say anything for a moment, so he just put his hand over her small one and nodded his thanks.

She smiled suddenly, brightly. 'See you in the morning, cowboy!'

26

She wheeled her pony and sent him skittering out of the yard, and Jim stood looking after her until a dip in the range hid her from view. Then he squared his shoulders and went into the house.

His father and mother were in the front room; she was darning socks and John Lawson was looking at a paper, although Jimmie was sure he wasn't reading. In an effort to divert their thoughts he began talking enthusiastically of the plan for trapping the black stallion. His father became interested and laid aside the paper; he seemed to welcome the diversion. They discussed plans and decided just how to build the barrier and where they would get the timber for it.

Outside, the darkness gathered and Mrs. Lawson lighted a lamp. They did not hear footsteps; they had no indication that a visitor was about to drop in on them. There came the soft click of the back door latch, then a man slipped into the kitchen and closed the door behind him. He said, 'Howdy, folks.'

It was too dark for them to distinguish his features, but they knew that voice.

It was the Kid who had entered.

CHAPTER THREE

EXILE

Jim saw his mother stiffen in her chair, saw the whiteness come into her face; then the sewing basket fell from her lap and she got up quickly and went towards the Kid.

'Edward!'

The Kid moved forward to meet her; he took her in his arms and kissed her. Jim got to his knees and absently started to pick up the articles spilled from the sewing basket.

John Lawson said, 'What are you doin' here, Ed? Are you plumb crazy?'

The Kid grinned at him over his mother's head. 'No; I'm smart. Tom Payne caught me here once, he won't figure on me comin' back again. I watched from the top of the mesa; the posse rode towards Springwater and he was with 'em. Got somethin' to eat, Mom? I'm starved.'

John Lawson got to his feet. 'You can't stay here,' he said harshly. 'You ought to know that. You've brought disgrace enough on us. Get somethin' to eat and then get out.'

'Now, John!' Mrs. Lawson protested.

'Nellie, I mean it. I'll not shelter him from

the law even if he is our son. He's forfeited every claim he had on us. He's a thief and worse. Today he killed another man. Yes, another! Tom Payne didn't tell you, but when he broke out of the courthouse he shot Ben Turner.'

'Ben had it comin',' said the Kid coldly. 'And I gave him his chance. I let him pull his gun.'

'And then shot him through the middle so he'd suffer!'

'I shot him through the middle because I didn't have time to get my gun any higher. I tell you he's had it comin' for months— tauntin' me about hangin' and sayin' he'd play the fiddle while I danced.'

The eyes were flaming yellow again.

'It was you that had it comin'!' blazed his father. 'You with your holdups and killin's! And now you escape your just punishment and we take it for you. Your mother and Jimmie and me. Folks look at us like we were dirt, and we have to beg Jeb Culpepper to let us buy food. The only man in town that's friendly is the one who should hate us most— Tom Payne. And I'm not insultin' that friendship by harborin' a criminal it's his duty to capture. Go now and eat, and then get out.'

The Kid stood watching him, his face stony. He said, 'All right; I'll eat and go. Fix

29

me somethin', Mom.'

He released her and Mrs. Lawson hurried to the cupboard. The Kid barred the back door and sat down at the table, and when she would have lighted the lamp he shook his head and said, 'No, Mom. There's light enough.' She went to the stove, and in the front room John Lawson sat down in his chair and picked up the paper. It was upside down and his hands shook as he held it.

Jimmie finished picking up the things that had fallen on the floor. His sympathies were divided; he was young enough to feel admiration for a man with the courage and daring of his brother and old enough to understand that his father's anger was justified. He put the sewing basket on a chair and walked slowly into the kitchen and sat down near his brother.

The Kid gave him a crooked smile. 'Stick to the straight and narrow, Jim,' he said. 'It ain't very excitin' and you'll never get rich, but at least you can eat your meals at home.'

Jimmie asked, 'Why did you shoot those men, Ed?'

The Kid looked pained. 'Why, because I had to, Jim. Think I did it just to hear my gun go off? And I didn't plug any of 'em in the back. They had their chance, all of them. Two were deputies who'd swore they'd get me. Art

Fenton yanked a gun from under the counter and woulda drilled me in another second. Ben Turner was all set to get me if I looked at him cross-eyed, even if I was ironed.'

Jimmie nodded. He could understand a man shooting another to preserve his own life; that was the code of the West in which he had been born. But the knowledge remained that his brother would not have had to shoot at all had he been engaged in a legal enterprise. It was hard for a boy of seventeen to judge.

The Kid said, 'I seen a beauty of a black stallion up on the mesa.'

Jim's face brightened with interest. 'I know. Nancy Payne said she saw him, too. Nancy and me have been chasin' him off and on for a year, and now we got it figured out how to catch him.'

He went on to describe their plan, and the Kid listened tolerantly, a sympathetic grin on his lips.

'You crowd him down into that canyon mouth and he'll fight,' he warned. 'He'll come at you all hoofs and teeth, and the one that ain't busy dodgin' him had better be ready to flip the noose over his neck in a hurry. Ain't nothin' can fight like a cornered stallion. I'd rather tackle a mountain lion any day.'

'We ain't afraid. Nancy can toss a rope with any man in the country; she'll snub

31

him down *pronto.*'

'Nancy Payne?' The Kid looked doubtful. 'She wasn't but a kid of ten when I saw her last. No bigger'n a minute. And homely as sin.'

'She ain't homely! She's beautiful.'

The Kid's grin widened and Jim colored uncomfortably.

'Well,' he amended, 'maybe not beautiful, but she ain't homely. Not any more. She's grown up since you seen her.'

'Sure. All of fourteen, ain't she? Girls grow a lot between ten and fourteen. She must have, to be ready to tackle a thousand pounds of hossflesh.'

He stopped abruptly and raised his hand for silence. He had stiffened, his leg muscles tensed to lift him from the chair. His head was cocked alertly towards the barred door.

Jim listened. Ham was sputtering in the frying pan, but above the sizzling sounds it made he thought he heard the stealthy tread of feet. Then the door latch rattled and a voice called, 'Open up!'

It was the voice of Sheriff Payne!

The Kid got up. He was wearing his gun this time, and his hand went quickly to its walnut butt and stayed there. His gaze was on the door. Mrs. Lawson turned sharply away from the stove and stood rigid, a hand pressed against her chest. Jimmie moved swiftly and softly around the table and stood beside his brother, a hand on the crooked arm as though to stay the Kid's draw. In the front room John Lawson got to his feet.

The voice came again. 'Open up! Ed Lawson, I want you. Come out quietly and don't make any trouble for your folks.'

The Kid's gun whipped out of its holster and leveled with its muzzle pointing at the door. Jimmie could see the dull glint of the barrel. He tugged at the Kid's arm.

'This way, Ed!' he whispered.

The Kid glanced at him with yellow eyes. Jimmie tugged again and jerked his head towards an adjoining room. 'This way. Please. Ed!'

The Kid backed away slowly, permitting Jim to guide him through a doorway into a small room which contained a chest of drawers, a chair and Jimmie's bed. Jim closed the door silently and tiptoed to a window. He looked through the pane, then tiptoed back to where the Kid stood.

'There's a man outside,' he whispered. 'Sheriff's probably got them all around the house. Ed, there's a trap-door in the ceilin' right over your head. Above it, in the roof is a scuttle. Remember? Get up on the roof and wait right over my window. Where's your horse?'

The Kid told him in a whisper. There was not much time. The back door remained barred, but evidently John Lawson had opened the front one, for they heard him call to Sheriff Payne to come in that way.

Jimmie set the chair in place under the trapdoor in the ceiling, and the Kid whispered, 'Thanks, Jim,' and got up on it. He pushed the trapdoor aside, gave a quick lifting bound and wiggled through the opening and into the attic. Jimmie replaced the chair even as the Kid put the trapdoor over the opening.

Jimmie went out into the kitchen and closed the bedroom door behind him. His mother still stood by the stove and in the faint light which filtered in from the front room he could see the anxious question in her eyes. He nodded reassuringly and lighted the kitchen lamp.

Men were coming through the front doorway and two of them stepped into the kitchen. They had guns in their hands. They went about looking behind the stove and under the table and into the big cupboard. Jimmie unbarred the door and opened it and saw two men standing outside. Their guns covered him but when they recognized him they lowered them. They pushed past him

34

into the kitchen and he went outside.

He heard Sheriff Payne say, 'Better get Nell and the boy outside, John. Ed is hidin' somewhere in the house and there may be some shootin'.'

Jim moved slowly away from the house. There were more men out here, but they had heard the sheriff's order and did not stop him. When he was concealed from them by the gloom he turned and walked rapidly towards the clump of alders where the Kid had left his horse; when it was safe to do so, he ran.

He found the horse and mounted him and rode him slowly towards the house. Men were riding about and he was not conspicuous. He drew a white handkerchief from his pocket and glanced along the roof line. He saw a dark blot against the sky and knew it must be the Kid's head. He raised the handkerchief and slowly waved it back and forth, then returned it to his pocket and rode up to the guard who stood watch beside the bedroom window.

Jim swung off the horse and crowded the animal close to the cabin wall, holding it by the bridle. The Kid would be directly above him, he knew. The guard peered at him through the darkness and said, 'Oh, it's you. Better get away from here. Lead's apt to fly and I don't want you in my way. Go on; ride off somewhere and keep away

35

from the house.'

'And watch while you corner my brother and kill him,' said Jim. 'I won't do it. *All right, Ed!*'

Still clinging to the bridle with his left hand, he flung his right arm about the guard and gripped the man's hand and drew it behind him where he could not use the gun it held. The Kid rolled from the roof and dangled for a moment gripping the eaves. The guard cursed and struggled, trying to free his arm, and the horse moved about restlessly; but Jimmie clung to hand and bridle and the Kid dropped right into the saddle and snatched up the rein.

'Good work, Jim!' he said tersely. 'Turn me loose!'

Jim let go the bridle and the horse was off like a stone from a sling. The cursing guard brought his left fist up to Jim's chin in a fierce uppercut that staggered the boy, then spun about and twisted his gun hand free. He emptied the Colt into the shadows which had swallowed the Kid, but the rhythm of the hoofbeats was not broken and there was no cry of pain from the rider.

Men came running from within the house and from the yard in front. The guard explained profanely as he stuffed fresh cartridges into his gun. They swore at Jim and one of them struck him. He leaped at the fellow, but Sheriff Tom Payne flung an arm about him and restrained him.

'Easy, Jimmie,' he said, and the boy desisted.

'There'll be no more of that,' Payne told his men. 'Get your horses and start after Ed. Get goin'! The more time you waste on the boy the better he'll like it.'

That jarred them out of their rage and they ran for their horses.

Payne said, 'That was a crazy thing to do, son. I could toss you into the calaboose for it, but I won't. Sooner or later we'll get Ed, and I'm sort of glad we didn't have to shoot him here.'

He got his horse and rode after the posse and Jim went back into the house. His mother was sitting in a chair crying into her apron, but the tears were tears of relief, for when he came in she jumped up and hugged him fiercely. His father was pacing up and down the floor, a heavy frown on his face.

Jimmie said, 'I'm sorry if you're mad, Pop; but I couldn't see them shoot Ed down in front of us.' He added weakly, 'Maybe if he gets away he'll quit bein' bad.'

His father sat down and lowered his head into his hands; his mother got up and put away the dishes she had got out for Ed's meal.

Jim went outside again and listened to the dying sounds of pursuit. When he came in again his father said dully, 'I reckon we'd better go to bed.'

They didn't sleep; each lay in bed and stared at the dark ceiling, taut of nerve and tortured with anxiety. They heard stealthy noises outside the house but did not investigate, thinking that some of the posse had come back to search the brush for Ed. It was the smell of smoke and the sudden glare of flames that got them up. They found one whole side of the cabin ablaze, and almost at once fire broke out in several other places. They put on some clothes and grabbed up buckets and ran for the spring, but they were licked from the start. Brush had been piled against the walls and set afire, and it was evident that the house was doomed.

Hurriedly they carried out what they could salvage, then stood at a distance watching while their home was consumed. They did not have to ask who had done it; some of the possemen had returned to mete out what they considered just punishment.

Jim did not meet Nancy the next morning. He was busy the whole day helping round up their cattle. Nancy's father sent his whole crew over to help, and the work continued through Monday. They gathered what stock they could as quickly as possible, not bothering to comb the foothills and the adjacent Payne range. On Tuesday they loaded what they had saved from the fire into the big freighting wagon. Mrs. Lawson drove it; Jim and his father and a couple of hands lent them by Tom Payne drove the cattle.

Nancy helped them until her father's men made her turn back. She tried not to cry as she said good-by to Jimmie, but her eyes were bright with tears.

'You'll be coming back some day, won't you, Jimmie?' she pleaded. 'We—we got to catch that black stallion, you know.'

'Yes, Nancy, I'll be comin' back.' His young face was tense with purpose. 'The land is ours; Pop proved up on it and they can't take it away from us. You—you sort of keep an eye on it for us. And when I come back we'll trap that black rascal and break him to carry double. So long.'

He rode swiftly away to overtake the slowly moving herd, and she sat her pony watching until the dust of the drag swallowed him. Then she slid from the saddle and hugged her pony fiercely and cried into his mane.

CHAPTER FOUR

RETURN

They pressed eastward, averaging from ten to fifteen miles a day, searching for suitable range and finding it at the end of two weeks. The cattle were gaunt and the Lawsons' dog tired, for, unwilling to take further advantage of Tom Payne's generosity, they had sent the Tepee riders home after the first week.

Their toil did not end when they finally let the weary cattle spread over the floor of the valley, for they must have corrals and sheds and a house in which to live. They felled trees which grew on the slopes of the hills and trimmed them and cut them to length and dragged them to the site they had selected, and in time a structure grew and took shape and became a house.

Mrs. Lawson worked along with them, sawing timber and driving nails in addition to providing for their physical comfort. She and Tom Lawson slept in the wagon until the house was finished, and Jim wrapped himself in his blankets and bedded down beneath it.

Months of privation followed. The nearest town was fifty miles away and four days were required for the round trip when supplies were needed. Their funds ran low and they could afford only the barest of necessities. Once during the first winter they were snowbound for days and actually suffered from hunger before John Lawson could break through on horseback and fetch in enough food to give them temporary relief.

On their trips to Hartsville for supplies, Jim and his father listened avidly for news of the Kid. They learned that he was still at large and operating in an adjoining state. His gang had grown to eight and they were specializing in train robbery now. After news of each fresh exploit, John Lawson's face would grow more haggard and grim and there would be little conversation on the return trip.

A year passed, two years, with little perceptible change. Jim grew older, stronger, wider of shoulder, a somber boy of nineteen. The third year saw them over the hump; the cattle had increased in number and grown fat on the lush range, prices went up, and the Lawsons could afford little luxuries that had been denied them before. They hired two elderly punchers who didn't mind the solitude and who lightened their tasks immeasurably.

But the third year also saw the beginning of the decline in health of Mrs. Lawson. She had worked beside her men uncomplainingly, and now that they had begun to reap the harvest of their toil she slowly began to fade. Jim and his father helped with the washing and the housework and finally took over altogether. At the end of the fourth year she passed away. Jim was now twenty-one.

A month after the funeral he told his father, 'I'm going back to Redrock. The ranch is ours and I aim to work it. Reckon I'll start in the morning.'

His father nodded without saying anything. He had known that Jim would go back some day and at times he wished he was younger so that he could go with him. But he was tired and his spirit had been broken.

Jim stuffed his saddlebags with food, tied his bedroll behind the cantle of his saddle and set out. During the four years of his exile the promise he had made Nancy to return had grown from a resentful impulse to a definite resolve. He would live down the bad reputation so recklessly built up by his brother Ed and demonstrate even to the most skeptical that one black sheep doesn't make a flock.

He made the trip in a bit over three days, camping the third night some ten miles west of Redrock, and rode into town the next morning. His blood warmed at the sight of familiar things—the dusty, crooked street, the shops and saloons, Jeb Culpepper's store—all the same as they had been four years before except for a little more grime, a little less paint, a slightly heightened appearance of dilapidation.

There were people on the street whom he recognized but who gave him no more than a casual glance; there were others who, after that first look, stopped to stare. The hard looks didn't embarrass him; he wanted them to know he was back. He wasn't ashamed of his appearance; his clothes were serviceable and neat, his horse was as good as any in Redrock and his rig was sturdy and handsome without being ornate. There was a rifle in the boot under his leg and a .45 Colt in the handtooled belt about his waist, and he was expert in their use. He was determined to resort to them only in an extreme emergency, for one careless shot would brand him with the same stamp that marked his brother.

He tied at Jeb Culpepper's store and went inside. There was nothing that he really needed but he wanted Jeb to know that he was back. The store was just as he remembered it; lanterns and watering pots and horse collars and harness hung from the rafters, the row of white bowls and pitchers still marched along the top shelf, the cracker box and molasses barrel stood in their accustomed places, the fly-specked candy case had its usual assortment of fingerprints on its glass.

Even Jeb was unchanged except for a little more whiteness about the temples. His lips were just as thin and his sharp eyes as mean as ever. He halted in his tracks when he recognized Jim and said, 'You, huh?'

'Yes. How are you, Jeb? I'd like a sack of Durham.'

For a moment Jeb hesitated, studying him, debating whether or not to serve him; but Jim returned his gaze steadily and Jeb finally got the tobacco and laid it on the counter.

'Just passin' through?' he asked.

'No. I've come back to stay.'

'Don't reckon you'll be very welcome.'

'Reckon not; but I'm here.'

'There's some mail-order catalogues come for you after you left. They're layin' around somewhere. Wait here and I'll get them.'

He went around the partition to the section of the store that was the post office and Jim made a cigarette and lighted it, leaning against the counter to smoke it. He thought he heard the back door open and close. A couple of minutes later he heard the squeak of hinges again, and Jeb came from behind the partition carrying several dusty catalogues.

'Here they are. Four years out of date, but I kept 'em.'

44

They were of no value now, but Jim was determined to lean backwards if necessary to avoid giving offense, so he thanked Jeb and took them with him. He got on his horse and rode out of town and when he had passed the last house he tossed them into the brush beside the road.

He rode slowly. It was familiar range upon which he gazed, and he thought of Nancy as he had thought of her many times during the years. She would be eighteen now. Had she remembered her old playmate? And the black stallion, was he still roaming the mesa?

A long ridge hid the Lazy L buildings from him and he urged his horse to its top anxious for that first look. The house was gone, of course, and the corrals and outbuildings would be in need of repair, but he yearned to see them as one yearns to see the face of a friend after a long absence.

The horse breasted the rise and he saw; and after that one startled look he halted the animal abruptly and the expression on his face changed from one of pleased anticipation to dawning apprehension.

A new house had grown upon the ashes of the old, a low, rambling house of logs with a huge stone chimney. Corrals and buildings were spick-and-span, newly whitewashed. There were horses in the corral and men

45

outside the bunkhouse. Somebody had squatted on the Lazy L!

Jim's jaws tightened and he urged the horse forward at a run. When he rounded the near corral he drew down to a walk and headed towards the house. Two men were standing on the low gallery and he recognized one of them at once. He was Dave Culpepper, bigger and broader now and his mustache full blown. He wore a rather fancy cowman's outfit and he was watching Jim with a hand on his pearl-handled Colt.

Jim drew rein before the gallery and returned Dave's hard stare. He said, 'Am I mistaken, or is this the Lawsons' Lazy L?'

'You're mistaken,' said Dave curtly. 'This was the Lawsons' Lazy L but it's the Culpepper's Circle C now.'

'You can't make that stick, Dave.'

'I figure I can. The Lawsons lost their right to this place when they helped a killer escape the law.'

'As long as my father holds the deed to the ranch he owns it. You can't take a man's property away from him just because his son broke the law.'

'That's what you think. Ain't anybody around here agrees with you. The people of Redrock decided four years ago that they could get along right well without the

Lawsons. They haven't changed their minds none.'

'Maybe the law will change it for them.'

'The law won't change a damned thing for the simple reason that if you go runnin' to court it'll be open season on all Lawsons. I got six good boys and they like it here. Look 'em over.'

Jim looked them over, starting with the one who stood beside Dave. He was slim, middle-aged, hard-faced, and looked more like a killer than Ed Lawson ever would. His eyes were green and so sharp that Jim could feel their stab. He let his eyes go over the others and got from each a cold hostile stare. There wasn't a pleasant look in the bunch and Jim doubted if they even joked among themselves.

'And now,' said Dave, 'you can start layin' down tracks.'

Jim nodded and turned his horse and walked him out of the yard. Quarreling with Dave Culpepper would gain him nothing but a possible bullet. Anger stirred him but he did not allow it to sway his judgment. He would take the matter to Sheriff Payne; Dave was trespassing and the sheriff had the power to evict him. Dave could tear down the house and carry it away log by log; he could move his cattle and scrape the whitewash from corrals and buildings; but he couldn't take the

Lawson range.

His gaze went to the north, in which direction lay the Tepee. He wanted to see Nancy again but was sure the sheriff would not bc at home. It would probably be necessary for him to ride to Springwater to see Tom, but he would try Redrock first. His meeting with Nancy must be postponed until later.

Back in Redrock he rode directly to the marshal's office, for it was here that he would find Payne if he were in town. News of his return had spread and the people he passed eyed him sullenly. Nobody spoke to him and he wasted no words in greeting them. He dismounted in front of the marshal's office, opened the door and went in.

There were two men in the office. One of them was Redrock's marshal, a man named Cliff Wood. He had been marshal as long as Jim could remember. The other was the guard Jim had tangled with that night outside his window when he had helped his brother escape. His name, Jim remembered, was Sydney Randall. They stared at him and Cliff Wood said, 'What do you want?'

'I'm looking for Sheriff Payne; know where I can find him?'

'He's out on the Tepee. He ain't sheriff no more.'

48

The news rocked Jim, but he tried not to show it. 'Who is?'

'I am,' answered Syd Randall. 'I run against Tom right after you left and beat him. I don't mind admittin' that you was my best backer. He had the Kid all wrapped up in a bundle that night and you opened the bag and let him out. Tom should have tossed you in jail, but he didn't and folks didn't like that. Much obliged to you.'

'Seeing that you're in my debt, you can pay off right now. Dave Culpepper's squatted on the Lazy L; you can run him off.'

'Maybe I can, but I won't. I'll pay that debt by advisin' you to push on your reins and keep goin' right out of the country before somebody hurts you. Folks haven't forgot the Kid and you ain't noways popular around here.'

'Dave is trespassing; it's your job to run him off.'

'A sheriff's allowed some discretion. Tom used his when he let you go; I'm usin' mine by refusin' to run Dave Culpepper off.'

'That goes double here,' said Marshal Wood.

Jim gave him a cold stare. 'You got nothing to do with it, Cliff. Your authority doesn't go beyond the town of Redrock.'

He turned and walked out of the office.

49

There was a sign across the street that had not been there when he left Redrock. It read, GARSON METCALF, Counselor at Law. Jim walked across and went into the office.

A man sat behind a desk trying to look busy. He was blond and neat and somewhere in his late twenties, Jim judged. When Jim came in he got up and nodded and said, 'Good morning, sir. Have a chair.'

Jim sat down in front of the desk. 'Mr. Metcalf, I'm James Lawson. My father owns the ranch where Dave Culpepper has squatted.'

He sensed rather than saw the other freeze. 'Lawson, eh? Are you related to Edward Lawson, the outlaw?'

'His brother. We moved away from Redrock four years ago, and while we were gone Dave Culpepper built a house and settled on our Lazy L. I saw him today and he refuses to leave. I want you to take whatever legal steps are necessary to put him off our property.'

Metcalf's lip tightened and he shook his head. 'Sorry, Lawson, but I can't take the case.'

'You're a lawyer, aren't you?'

'I am, and I expect to remain in Redrock. I've heard of you. If I were to represent you I might as well close shop. And you don't need

50

a lawyer. The sheriff has authority to evict trespassers.'

'The sheriff,' said Jim tightly, 'has also heard of me.' He got up.

Metcalf came around the desk and followed him to the door.

'Nothing personal about this, Lawson. You can see my position. I just can't afford to have you for a client. No hard feelings, I hope.'

'Not at all, Mr. Metcalf. They say jellyfish have no backbones and sometimes I feel sorry for them, but I never expected to meet one. Good morning.'

He went out leaving Metcalf frowning in the doorway.

His jaws were tightly clamped as he crossed the street to his horse. Undoubtedly there was a conspiracy on foot to keep him away from Redrock. He knew that Jeb Culpepper had slipped out the back way when he was supposed to be getting the mail-order catalogues and had sent word out to his son. Syd Randall, the sheriff, had anticipated Jim's appeal and had made his decision before he had heard Jim's complaint. It was likely that Metcalf had been tipped off as to the course of action to take.

The feeling of frustration was strong; Syd Randall was a power in Springwater, the county seat, and would do everything he could

51

to block Jim's efforts to regain the Lazy L. The law was lax in this section and Jim would have found the going tough even if the Kid's identity had never been established. He had counted strongly on the aid of Sheriff Tom Payne; now that that prop was gone the future looked anything but rosy.

He was about to step into his saddle when Marshal Wood came from his office and walked over to the hitching rack. His lips were tight and he was scowling. He said, 'You reminded me that my jurisdiction was limited to the town of Redrock. Remember that and don't come back to town.'

'Cliff, you know you can't forbid my coming to Redrock as long as I obey the law.'

'I can and I am. You're a disturbin' influence; sooner or later somebody's goin' to start a fight with you. It's my job to keep the peace and I figure it'll be a heap easier to do if you stay away from town. Now mount up and ride and don't come back.'

Sheriff Randall had come to the office door and was watching narrowly.

Jim choked back the angry protest and got into his saddle. For the present he had to take anything they dished out. He rode slowly down the street.

CHAPTER FIVE

'GET 'EM UP—
AND EMPTY!'

Jim pondered his problem as he rode out of town. The ranch was his father's but the sheriff had refused to help him and his only recourse was the law. He came to the fork in the road which led to Springwater and turned into it, riding rapidly and halting at noon near a spring to eat and rest his horse. It was midafternoon when he rode into the county seat.

Here he was not known and would not readily be associated with the Kid who had escaped from the courthouse four years before. He picked out a lawyer at random and explained what he wanted done. The attorney, a grave-faced man with bushy hair and sideburns who bore the name of Newton Kling, said there should be no difficulty in getting a court order which Sheriff Randall would be forced to serve, and told Jim to be on hand at nine in the morning.

Jim went to the hotel, engaged a room, then stabled his horse and took a chair on the veranda. He had read accounts of his brother's escape and now he gazed interestedly at the courthouse, diagonally across the street and at the restaurant from which Ben Turner had walked to meet the Kid's bullet.

As the supper hour approached, men who took their meals at the hotel began to assemble on the veranda. Lawyer Kling took a chair beside Jim's and the two conversed casually for a while; then a horseman pulled up at the hitching rack and Jim recognized Sheriff Randall. He came up on the veranda, exchanging greetings with several of the men, caught sight of Jim and the lawyer and came over to look at them.

He said to Kling, 'Like to talk with you a minute, Newt.'

Kling got up and walked away with him and they stood talking until the supper bell clanged. They went into the dining room and continued the conversation during the meal, and Jim knew that the sheriff was trying to persuade the lawyer to give up the case.

Jim finished supper and went back to the veranda. The town was waking up now; miners from near-by claims were coming in and a bunch of cowboys swept by in a race for the Gold Standard, Springwater's most popular gambling and drinking emporium.

Jim had been seventeen when he left Redrock and the four years which followed had been spent on a lonely ranch fifty miles from a town. The crowd on the street, the constant movement, the subdued sounds of conversations and clinking glasses and coins with their background of distant mechanical music fascinated him. The hours drifted by and at last he descended the steps and started to make a circuit of the town.

The sounds from within the Gold Standard attracted him and he went inside. On his left was a bar which extended almost the length of the room; down the center paraded the gambling layouts; along the wall to his right were tables and chairs; at the far end of the place was a stage with a piano in front of it. The stage was lighted and a girl was singing. Jim got a glass of beer and carried it to an obscure table and sipped it as he watched.

The girl was a blonde with plenty of curves and she wore a sleeveless evening gown of yellow from beneath which peeped the tips of golden slippers. She laughed at the crowd as she sang and they roared their approval.

The song finished, she came down from the stage and was immediately surrounded by a cluster of men. She refused their offers of drinks and they drifted away one by one as she moved slowly along the aisle between gaming tables and bar. She was glancing alertly about her and finally saw Jim. She came towards him, a smile on her lips, and he instinctively got to his feet and removed his hat, blushing with embarrassent. She was a dance-hall girl, but she was a woman and he had been taught to respect women.

'You look lonely,' she said. 'Would you like to buy me a drink?'

'Yes, ma'am, I sure would.'

She slipped gracefully into a chair on the opposite side of the table and said, 'I'll have a glass of beer.'

Jim nodded and crossed to the bar. He bought two beers and carried them to the table and put one before her. 'Here's luck,' she wished him, and sipped slowly.

He sat down and gravely responded. She was observing him curiously.

'You're a stranger, aren't you?'

'Sort of. I lived in Redrock four years ago, but we—left—right after Ed Lawson escaped from the courthouse. I'm Jim Lawson, Ed's brother.'

He did not lower his gaze; he would not cringe before anybody.

Interest widened her eyes. 'Is that so? I've heard about the Kid. He's a brave man, and a lucky one.' She glanced about quickly, then spoke in a lowered voice. 'Are you going to meet him here?'

'No, ma'am. I came back to reclaim the

Lawson ranch. Ed's not even in this state.'

'Oh, but he is! He and his gang held up a train at Junction City just last week. That's in this state and not more than thirty miles away.'

The news stunned him. 'I didn't know that. You're sure it was Ed?'

'Of course. His gang still wear masks but they're well known. If I were you I'd keep quiet about being Jim Lawson. You remember Ben Turner? His cousin, Hal, owns the Gold Standard. That's him over there in the cashier's cage.'

Jim looked in the direction she indicated and saw a booth at the far end of the bar. Inside the heavy grill-work sat a man big enough and tough enough to do his own bouncing. He wore a bushy mustache and eyebrows to match.

Jim looked back at the girl. 'I'm not ashamed to let people know who I am. My idea in coming back is to make people respect the name of Lawson in spite of what Ed has done. I aim to tend to business and bother nobody.'

'Do you think they'll let you?' Her lips were twisted cynically. 'They'll pick at you and hurt you every way they can and finally you'll go on the prod and they'll say you're just as bad as your brother.'

'Maybe. I'm going to risk it.'

'Yes, I guess you will. If your brother had stayed out of the state you might have had a chance; but now folks are stirred up again and they won't let you make good no matter how you try.'

Jim frowned at his glass. She was probably right. Why did Ed have to pick this time to return? Why couldn't he have waited until Jim had had a chance to establish himself? He understood now the refusal of Garson Metcalf to take his case; the bitter animosity of Marshal Cliff Wood and Sheriff Syd Randall was explained. He shook off his depression and looked up at her.

'Would you like another drink, Miss—?'

'Roselle. Nesta, to you. No thanks, Jim. Or should I say Jimmie? I think I like Jimmie.' She got up. 'I've got to circulate around the joint and earn my pay. I'll be seeing you, Jimmie.' Once more she lowered her voice. 'If you gamble, let the dice and faro alone.'

She gave him a smile and a pert nod and moved away. He had risen and now stood looking interestedly after her. Nesta Roselle; too pretty a name to be her own. But she certainly hadn't acted as he thought a dance-hall girl should act. She wasn't coarse and blatant and she had refused the second drink he had offered to buy. It was swell of her to

58

warn him against games which were probably crooked. Why had she done it?

Nesta was asking herself the same question. He was a stranger and she had approached him deliberately to find out if he had any money. If he had, it was her duty to coax him to the roulette wheel where he would be permitted to win; from there she would steer him to the dice and faro tables where he would promptly be separated from his winnings and as much of his own cash as he could be persuaded to part with. Instead of doing this she had ordered the cheapest drink, and had warned him against the games where he must surely lose. It bothered her.

He's such a nice boy, she told herself. *It must be the mother instinct in me. I'm getting old and sentimental.*

Jim drank his beer, watching her through the crowd. He saw her speak to a bearded, flannel-shirted miner who flung an arm around her and drew her towards the roulette wheel. Jim got up and walked over to watch. The miner had a stack of chips and played them as Nesta indicated. She did not glance at Jim, appearing absorbed in the play.

She played the various combinations, just about breaking even. At last she said, 'This is too slow, honey; let's put a stack on a number, huh?'

'Anything you say, baby. I'm ridin' high tonight. What number?'

She studied the layout, then put a finger on 28. 'This one.'

The miner put a stack of ten chips on 28 and the dealer spun the wheel.

'More!' cried Nesta, and pushed a second stack out on the board.

A sudden hunch hit Jim. He had no chips, but he drew a ten-dollar gold piece from his pocket and put it on 28. The dealer gave him a quick look, but the wheel was turning and the ball had been tossed. It rolled around the rim, then settled lower as the speed slackened. Just before the wheel stopped it popped into 28 and remained there.

'Whoop-eee!' cried the miner. 'Talk about a lucky lady!' He threw his arms about Nesta and gave her a bear hug. She looked over his shoulder directly at Jim and he saw her brows draw together in a little frown and thought that she shook her head ever so slightly at him. He could not be sure; the frown might have been the result of the miner's roughness, the shake of the head a wince of pain. but Jim had the distinct feeling that a warning had been flashed to him.

He looked down to see a huge pile of chips in front of him. He continued to play, but his bets were conservative and did not follow

Nesta's choices. He lost, but the miner lost also, and finally Nesta said, 'Our luck's run out here, honey; let's try some dice.'

The miner agreed. 'Whatever you say, baby.' He gathered up his chips and permitted her to lead him to the dice layout.

Jim took his chips to the cashier's cage and exchanged them for money, then strolled over to the dice layout to watch the miner play. He lost steadily, and finally Nesta steered him to the faro table. Here what chips he had remaining quickly went. He drew a buckskin poke from his hip pocket and plunked it on the table. 'Weigh her up and give me chips,' he said.

'I'll get them from the cashier,' Nesta told him, and carried the poke to the cage.

'*Hold everything, folks!*'

The order rang out above the din of conversation and the clink of glass and coin, and brought a surprised silence. Eyes sought the source of the voice, found it and remained fixed. Three men had come into the room; they were masked and there were guns in their hands. One of them stood just beside the doorway; the second moved to a corner where he could watch the bar and gaming tables; the third, he who had given the order, stood at the head of the gambling layout.

Jim stared at this man, and there was a

61

sensation at the pit of his stomach as though he had received a blow in the solar plexus. It had been four years since he had heard that voice but he knew it instantly. It was the voice of his brother, the Kid.

From the rear came another order. *'Get 'em up—and empty!'*

Heads pivoted in that direction. Three more masked men had entered by a door at one side of the stage. One of them remained at the doorway, a second had mounted to the stage where he could command the crowd, the third was striding towards the cashier's cage. It was he who had given the order, and it was directed at Hal Turner.

He repeated, 'I said to get 'em up!' and there was a double click as he drew back the hammer of the threatening Colt. Hal Turner glared at him for a few seconds, then slowly raised his hands shoulder-high.

'Unlatch the door and come out.' Then to Nesta, who was standing before the grille, 'Step aside, lady.'

Nesta moved back a few paces, her curious gaze on the bandit. Turner, after a short hesitation, unlatched the door and backed out.

The Kid had been advancing steadily, his companions covering his movements. He was watching Hal Turner but something brought his attention to Jim. He stopped dead and Jim caught the glint of eyes through the holes in the mask and knew that Ed had recognized him.

The Kid passed on, and now he was watching Nesta. He stopped before her and she held out the poke of gold. 'I guess you want this,' she said.

The Kid raised his hat. 'You wrong me, Miss. We never rob ladies. Especially pretty ones. I'd settle for a kiss but I haven't the time.'

He stepped past her, his gaze once more on Hal Turner, and Nesta shrugged her shoulders in wonderment and lowered the sack of gold. The Kid ordered Hal into a corner, then while his men kept Turner covered he entered the cage and swiftly scooped all the money into a canvas sack. When he had cleaned out the cage he went behind the bar and emptied the tills. He did not bother with the games, for while there was some money in sight most of the play was with chips and the Kid, as usual, was depending upon surprise and speed for a successful cleanup and getaway.

Carrying the heavy sack, the Kid crossed to the rear door and turned to speak shortly. 'Everything stay put for three minutes. If a head shows outside the door, it gets popped.'

The holdup was perfectly organized. The two men at the front came quickly along the side wall and went out through the rear doorway. The three who had entered that way followed them. The Kid backed to the door, his gun holding the crowd; he backed into the passageway and pulled the door shut after him. The door clicked.

There came a bull-like roar from the end of the bar and Jim turned his head to look. Hal Turner, face red and eyes bulging, had seized a sawed-off shotgun and was moving with long strides towards the back door. The Kid's warning was ignored; he yanked open the door and leaped out with gun leveled, waist-high.

A shot boomed and he staggered, then came a mighty blast as his fingers tightened convulsively on the shotgun triggers. He turned and stumbled through the doorway and collapsed on the floor.

Men ran towards him. He pushed himself to hands and knees then fell again. This time he lay still. They rolled him over and saw that a bullet had gone into his chest. A doctor lived across the street but nobody seemed willing to venture outside the place.

'I'll get him,' said Nesta, and started for the front door.

They called to her to wait the three minutes

out, but she tossed her head disdainfully. 'If they won't rob a lady they certainly won't shoot one,' she said, and pushed through the swinging doors. She returned almost at once with the doctor. The three minutes were up but nobody else had moved out of the saloon.

'It's bad,' pronounced the doctor when he had finished his examination, 'but he has a chance. We'll get him in bed.' He turned to a bartender. 'Better close up the place; Hal will need quiet.'

Some of them carried the unconscious man from the room; the others filed quietly out of the place. They were talking in low tones and Jim heard what some of them said.

'It was the Kid, wasn't it?'

'Yeah. Wonder how much he got?'

'If Hal cashes his chips he'll be—Say! How many *has* the Kid killed?'

'Well, Ben was the fourth and he's rubbed out two since. Hal'd make the seventh. If they ever catch up with the Kid they oughta burn him at the stake.'

Jim felt a hand on his arm and turned his head to see Nesta standing beside him. 'Some lad, that brother of yours,' she whispered. 'I wish he'd had more time.'

Jim's feet dragged as he passed through the doorway to the street.

CHAPTER SIX

BEHIND THE MESS SHACK

There was much bustle and confusion in the street. It seemed that everybody in town had gathered before the Gold Standard, talking excitedly, gesturing. Sheriff Syd Randall pushed through the crowd; he caught sight of Jim and for one instant let him have the full benefit of his angry glare, then shouted loudly for order.

When he had their attention he said, 'I want a big posse and I want it in a hurry. Everybody that's got a hoss saddle up and meet me in front of the courthouse. If you ain't totin' a rifle you can get one there.'

The crowd broke up, each man running for his horse or weapons. Randall started back along the sidewalk, but halted momentarily in front of Jim.

'I've a danged good mind to take you in,' he said tersely. 'You're his brother and it's my hunch that you had somethin' to do with this holdup.'

'You're off your range, Randall. I didn't even know Ed was in the state.'

66

'Like fire you didn't! But I got no time to waste on you now.'

He went down the street towards the courthouse and Jim walked slowly to the hotel. He went into the hotel lobby, found it deserted except for the night clerk, and sat in a chair by the big front window. The clerk glared at him from time to time and Jim knew that word of his relationship to the Kid had got around. He watched the posse sweep out of town, yipping with the excitement of the chase, then went to bed and lay pondering his problem. He had to stick it out, of course; if he left now he could never come back. It was a long while before he went to sleep.

They didn't catch the Kid that night. The posse came riding in for breakfast, weary and sleepy and glum. Syd Randall was red-faced and angry and Jim gave him a wide berth. At nine o'clock he went down to Lawyer Kling's office. Kling gave him a short good-morning and asked him to sit down.

The lawyer said, 'I've been thinking this matter over, Lawson, and I don't believe it would be wise to go to Judge Calder this morning. You aren't the actual owner of the Lazy L; it belongs to your father. I'm afraid the judge will insist that any trespassing charges be brought by the owner.'

'Which means?'

'There are three courses open to you. You can write your father to forward the deed to me, retaining me as his attorney; you can get your father's power of attorney authorizing you to act for him; or you can have him deed the property over to you, thus giving you the right to act.'

'In other words, I'm being given the royal run-around.'

'You're being given damned good legal advice,' snapped Kling. 'You know how you stand in this community. The ranch is legally your father's and he can regain possession through legal channels; but the people of Redrock and Springwater don't want any Lawsons around. Handling the case is going to hurt me, but I'll do it; but not until I can go before Judge Calder knowing that I can win it.'

'I see,' said Jim tightly, and got up. 'Good morning, Mr. Kling.'

He went back to the hotel and wrote a letter to his father asking him to transfer the ranch to him, then mailed it at the post office and returned to the hotel. He had paid for a day's meals and lodging and had dinner coming. Time was not crowding him; there was nothing he could do towards reclaiming the ranch until his letter was answered. That would take time, for his father would have to go to Hartsville in order to comply with the legal requirements, and mail connections between the two places were slow and uncertain. His next step would be to visit the Paynes. He would ask Tom's advice and he wanted very much to see Nancy.

He started for Redrock immediately after eating dinner and sighted the town late that afternoon. He rode through it and into the valley and cut across the range towards the Tepee.

The valley in which the two ranches were located lay between parallel mountain ranges which ran roughly from northwest to southeast. At the upper end and on the western side were the Tepee buildings; the Lazy L headquarters were situated at the foot of the same range but some five miles to the southeast. Between the Lazy L and the Tepee was the mesa where Jim and Nancy had planned to trap the black stallion.

A creek rose in the hills behind the Lazy L and originally ran due east across the valley and through a gap near Redrock, but Jim's father had diverted it after Tom Payne moved into the valley so that it now followed the middle of the valley and partly across Payne's ranch, dwindling with distance until it had finally disappeared.

The diversion was an act of friendliness on

Lawson's part, for without this water the Tepee range would be dry and worthless. Lawson was willing to share the water because he liked Tom Payne and wanted him for a neighbor. A fence crossed the valley, separating the two spreads. The old creek bed lay on the Lazy L side of the fence.

The Tepee appeared unchanged as Jim approached it, the log ranch house sprawling in its grove of cottonwoods, the outbuildings and corrals on either side and behind it. There seemed to be nobody about as Jim rode into the yard, but this was not unusual since Tom and his crew would probably be working on the range. Jim had hoped, though, to see Nancy.

He dismounted before the gallery, draped his rein over the hitching rail and called, 'Hello, the house!'

He got no answer, so he walked around the low gallery in time to see a man come out of the mess shack. He was bowlegged and bewhiskered and walked with a limp. He wore the same shabby, misshapen hat he had worn ever since Jim had known him. He came limping towards the house like a river steamboat with a broken paddlewheel, his lean jaws working rhythmically with his stride. His face was tanned to the color of weak coffee and he was as wrinkled as a dried russet apple, but his eyes were as black and sharp as the eyes of a ferret.

A dozen feet away from Jim he halted and stared and forgot to chew for a moment; then he exploded, 'Wal, I'll be a diddely-dad-burned son of a lop-eared lollapaloosa! Jimmie Lawson, you dad-ratted maverick! How the hell are yuh?'

He came forward, one bony hand extended, and Jim seized and wrung it.

'Limpy! Gosh, it's good to see you! Where's everybody?'

Limpy made a vague gesture. 'Out some'eres, workin'. Heerd you'd come back. Whatcha gonna do about Dave Culpepper, kick him off'n the Lazy L?'

'Going to put him off legally. It's the only way—now.'

'Yeah. The dad-ratted, pic-faced son of a biscuit! I wisht you could bust in there with a bunch of boys and blow 'em right outa the county. Heerd Ed went on another of his rampages last night.'

Jim sobered. 'Held up the Gold Standard and wounded Hal Turner.'

'Ed's a wild un. Allus was. Be a good thing for all the Lawsons if somebody'd plug him.'

'Maybe I should have let Tom Payne take him that night at the Lazy L,' said Jim miserably.

'Yore own brother? Don't you think it. I got no use for kinfolk that don't stand up for each other. No, sir, you done just right.' He squinted past Jim and towards Redrock. 'Here comes Nancy. Danged li'l brat allus rides like she had three minutes to make a train and the station four minutes away.'

Jim turned to look and saw two mounted figures rushing towards the ranch. The one in front was a girl, although at that distance he could not distinguish her features. Her hat had blown off and hung by the throat latch and her dusky hair streamed out behind her.

As she drew closer, details became visible. Jim saw that she was still slim and graceful, but more rounded and mature than the Nancy he had known. Her cheeks were pink with exercise and excitement, her eyes sparkled and her lips were parted. As she neared the house she pulled her pony down to a crowhop and turned in her saddle to call, 'I told you Princess could beat that gelding of yours.'

Not until then did Jim glance at the second rider, and when he did so he felt a little wave of resentment sweep over him. The horseman who followed her into the yard was Dave Culpepper. He was smiling, but there was a hint of malice in the smile. He said, 'It wasn't a fair start. You beat the gun.'

'I did not! Princess was just quicker on the

getaway.'

She reined her pony to a stop and when he had joined her they rode to the gallery side by side.

'I'll be a-seein' yuh,' Limpy told Jim in a low voice, and turned away. Jim flung the old fellow a quick glance and saw him spit in the dust. He did it viciously, as if he wished it were Dave he was spitting on. Jim went around the corner of the gallery and they saw him.

Nancy just stared for a moment, the color fading from her cheeks; then it returned with a rush and she flung herself from the saddle and came running to meet him, her hands extended.

'Jimmie! It *is* you, isn't it?'

He took her hands and held fast to them. They were warm and soft. He said, 'Yes, it's me, Nancy. Gosh, you look swell!'

'You too! Jimmie, why didn't you write?'

'I don't know, except that I always figured on coming back, and the time just went, and—' He shook his head. 'I just thought things could wait until I did.'

They stood there looking at each other, and he still held her hands. Dave Culpepper had dismounted and was standing beyond her. His face was blank except for his eyes. They smoldered.

She remembered him and turned, disengaging one of her hands but clinging to Jim with the other.

'Dave, you remember Jimmie, don't you?'

'Yeah, I remember him. We met yesterday. Didn't have much luck in Springwater, did you, Lawson?'

'No. But my luck will change when I get the deed from Father.'

'Lots can happen before then.'

Nancy said quickly, 'I've got to run into the house and start supper. You'll stay, of course, Jimmie. Dad'll want to see you. And you too, Dave.'

'Not me. I'll be amblin' along presently. Go right ahead, Nancy.'

She glanced doubtfully from one to the other of them, but they both gave her reassuring smiles and she turned and went into the house.

Dave said, 'You'll be putting your hoss in the corral. I'll walk along. There's somethin' I want to show you.'

Jim nodded and took the rein from the hitching rail and they walked together in silence to the corral.

'I'll wait till you put him up,' said Dave. 'What I want to show you is behind the mess shack.'

'Might as well take a look at it now. The

horse can wait.'

He looped the rein about a rail and followed Dave towards the mess shack. They rounded the corner. There was nothing here that hadn't been here four years ago, but Jim hadn't expected there would be. He thought he knew what was coming and his blood pounded hard in his veins. It came, but without the warning he had expected.

Dave pivoted swiftly, his right fist sweeping in a powerful arc with all his weight behind it. Jim threw up his left arm, but much too late. The fist struck him solidly on the temple. The blow jarred him to the soles of his feet and sent him staggering sideways; his spurs tangled and he fell beneath the mess-shack window. Instantly Dave's Colt whipped out and up. His face was a savage mask and he spat the words at Jim with the velocity of bullets.

'I been savin' that for you and I got more where it come from, I told you if you went to the law it would be open season on Lawsons. You can climb on your hoss and ride clear out of the state or you can stay and take what I aim to hand out to you. Now get up and get goin'.'

Jim pushed himself to a sitting position. The stars had stopped exploding but his head still whirled and his brain was numb from shock. He couldn't think coherently, but a red rage seethed in him and if there had been any power left in his muscles he would have leaped at Dave, gun and all.

'Come on,' ordered Dave viciously. 'Get up and git!'

A voice spoke from the opened mess-shack window. 'Put that hawglaig back in leather, you locoed son of a dad-ratted polecat!'

Jim glanced upward. A dragoon Colt slanted over the sill. It was almost as big as a sawed-off shotgun. It was pointed at Dave and behind it was Limpy. Dave was staring too, but his gun still covered Jim.

Limpy spoke again. 'I reckon you heard me, Dave. Put that hawglaig up or I'll try shootin' it outa your hand. If I do, you'll shore enough git some barked knuckles.'

Dave hesitated, his gaze still on Limpy, then let the muzzle of the Colt drop and slid the weapon into its holster.

'Now you can mount up and git!'

'Wait a minute, Limpy.' Jim got his feet under him and erected himself. 'Dave said he had some more of those punches. I liked the sample and want to see some more. Lay the gun aside, Dave, and we'll start over.'

He had unbuckled his gun belt while he spoke; now he wrapped it about the Colt and put it on the ground some ten feet away. As soon as he got Jim's meaning, Dave hurried to follow suit. His eyes were glinting with purpose and anticipation. He was twenty pounds heavier than Jim, and as a boy had beaten him at will. This was too good to be true.

There was no feinting, no sparring for openings; Dave came leaping forward with both arms swinging. They were vicious swings, each packing the kick of a mule, but they didn't land. They were deflected by a pair of strong forearms and Dave came to a sudden halt because he found himself chest to chest with a man who refused to give an inch before his rush. And now he was in too close for the flailing arms to do any good.

Hard fists pounded his midsection like a volley of rocks, and Dave grunted and groaned with agony. He couldn't take it and backed away, still throwing those futile haymakers. Jim ducked and set himself. When Dave was the proper distance away for maximum effect, he stepped forward and threw a right to the chin with everything in it he had. Dave went down, hard.

He sat there, supporting himself with one arm. He wasn't out, but there was a glaze over his eyes and his brain was dead. Jim watched, a fierce exultation gripping him. That was Dave Culpepper down there. Dave Culpepper, the boy who had taunted him and beaten him, the man who had stolen his father's ranch and had declared open season on Lawsons. He wasn't doing any taunting or beating now!

Limpy was shouting delightedly. 'Ho-lee jumpin' cowbells! If that wasn't a lollapaloosa! Pick yourself up and git goin', Dave. And don't forget I'll still be coverin' you while you pick up yore gun.'

Dave got slowly to his feet. His hat had fallen off; he stooped and mechanically picked it up, dusted it on his thigh and put it on his head. He didn't say a word, just buckled the belt about him with trembling fingers and moved away. He staggered slightly as he walked.

Jim put on his own gun belt and followed him to the corner of the mess shack to watch Dave mount and ride slowly away. Limpy joined him and was chuckling.

'Ain't enjoyed m'self so much since Bib Potter fell outa the hearse,' he declared. 'Jest a-seein' that made me twenty years younger.'

'I thought for a moment you'd have to shoot,' said Jim. 'I was wondering if you would.'

'Shoot? With that old dragoon Colt? Feller, it ain't been loaded since the Mexican War. And even if it was I couldn't a-fired it. The hammer's busted plumb off!'

CHAPTER SEVEN

ON THE MESA

Nancy came out of the house and watched Dave ride away, then hurried to the corral where Jim was stripping his horse. She was tense and anxious.

'Something happened between you and Dave, Jimmie. What was it?'

'He just wanted to show me something.'

Limpy spoke. 'It was a fist he showed Jimmie. He showed it to him when he wasn't lookin', the dad-ratted son of a cockeyed coyote! And then Jim showed him what great, big muscles he's got. And Dave set down on his hind end sorta suddenlike and looked up at 'em and decided he'd better go home. The dad-ratted son of a—son of a—!' Limpy couldn't find a word expressive enough, so he spat, viciously.

Nancy was delighted. 'You didn't really, Jimmie! Oh, good for you!'

Jim was puzzled. She and Dave had appeared on the best of terms, yet she gloried in Culpepper's defeat. He put the horse into the corral and walked back to the house with her. He went into the kitchen and sat down, and they talked while he watched her prepare supper.

'How long has he been on the Lazy L?'

'Over three years. He took over after Syd Randall was elected. We hadn't heard from you and Ed was raising hob in the next state and Dad not being sheriff gave him his chance. Dad and Randall weren't very friendly and Dad lost his pull at Springwater when he was defeated. There just wasn't anything we could do except gather what Lazy L cattle there were and look after them like you asked me to when you left.'

'That was swell of you, Nancy.'

'It was the least we could do. Dad turned them over to me and told me it was my job to look after them. They've grown into a nice little herd.'

His eyes shone. 'Nancy! All these years!'

Her cheeks were flushed but it may have been from the heat of the stove.

'It wasn't hard. I liked it. I sort of figured they were my own. There was some fine stock in the hills; we bred them carefully and you have nearly a hundred head of good cattle. I sold them off for beef when they were three years old and collected over a thousand dollars for you. It's in the bank in my name.'

'Nancy!' Gratitude welled up in him. He couldn't say any more.

She tossed her dusky curls. 'I wanted to show Dad that I savvied cows as well as the next one.'

'I'll tell a man you do! But it's a partnership proposition. Half of everything, stock and cash, is yours.'

'We'll argue about that later. What are you going to do about the Lazy L?'

'There's nothing I can do right now. Dave refuses to leave, Syd Randall won't put him off, the lawyer in Redrock says it would ruin him if he handled it for me, and Kling, in Springwater, tells me the charges against Dave must be brought by my father unless he transfers the ranch to me. They've got me hogtied all around.'

'If it wasn't for Ed it would be easy.' Sudden passion seized her. 'Oh, why did he have to come back? I should think he'd know he's done enough to hurt you.'

'He didn't know I was back. We hadn't heard from him since we left Redrock. He saw me in the Gold Standard and I thought for a minute he was going to talk to me. But he didn't. I reckon he knew it would look bad for me if he did.'

'Thank goodness he had that much sense! How're the folks?'

'Pop's pretty good, considering. Mom died a month ago.'

She turned swiftly. 'Oh, Jimmie, I'm so sorry!'

He hastened to change the subject. 'How about the black stallion? Is he still roaming the mesa?'

'No. It's funny, but right after you left he left, too. And he's never been back. I guess we'll never catch him now.'

The thud of hoofs came to them and she glanced through the window.

'Here come Dad and the boys now. Want to help me set the table?'

They bustled about the kitchen, setting places for three. They were putting on the finishing touches when Tom Payne came in. He stopped in the doorway to stare, then his big face brightened and he strode forward with a hand extended.

'Jimmie! Heard you were back and figured you wouldn't forget old friends. How's tricks, son?'

Jim wrung the hand. 'Not bad, Mr Payne. I wanted to see you before this but was kept sort of busy. How are you?'

'Tired, son. Tired and dirty. Wait just a minute and I'll wash up. Nancy, that sure smells good. You're nearly as good a cook as your ma was.'

'Jimmie just lost his mother too, Dad.'

'No! When?'

Jim told him and he said that sure was tough and went out shaking his head in sympathy. He washed and they sat down to a good dinner and talked as they ate. Jim told them what had happened since his arrival.

'I'm tied up until I get that deed from Pop,' he finished. 'I don't know what to do in the meantime. I thought maybe you could advise me, Tom.'

'Why, you'll stay right here with us,' said Payne heartily.

Jim shook his head. 'I don't want to. I'm poison. You befriended me once and lost the sheriff's job. Tom, I'm right sorry about that.'

'Forget it. Never did like sheriffin'. I'm a cowman. You stay here.'

'No. It's not as though I was broke and hungry. I'm not. I have some money and Nancy told me what she did with the Lazy L stock when we left. I'll never be able to repay you folks for that, and half of everything is yours. They don't want me in Redrock or Springwater, so I'll camp up on the mesa until I get that deed. I wrote Pop to send it to you. Jeb Culpepper's postmaster and I want to be sure to get it.'

'Good idea. Jeb's as crooked as a wolf's hind leg. But no need for you to camp on the mesa. Stay here, and if you feel obliged you

83

can work with my boys. They all know you and like you.'

'That's swell. That's sure swell.' Jimmie had to swallow hard. After the hatred and animosity he had met on every hand he had found friends and the knowledge stirred his emotion. 'But I still think I should go it alone. You can help me better if folks don't know about it.'

Payne stared at him thoughtfully. 'You might have something there.'

'I think he has,' said Nancy promptly. 'Not that we're afraid of what folks might think or say, but we can help. And that's what Jimmie needs; help, not sympathy.'

Tom asked, 'You got any ideas, son?'

'I didn't have when I came out here, but since Nancy told me about the cattle I got me a hunch. There's plenty of grazing land in or near the valley and I have quite a little cash. I could homestead a quarter-section and make my improvements. I can give it up when I get the Lazy L, unless I wanted to hang onto it.'

Nancy's eyes were bright. 'That's it, Jimmie! There's land right here in the valley open to homesteading.'

Payne also was enthusiastic. 'It's the right hunch, son. And here's somethin' else: legal machinery can move gosh-awful slow when the wrong engineer's at the throttle. Dave

84

might manage to string the thing out for a long time before you finally get rid of him. Instead of eatin' into your capital while you wait for a settlement, you could be raisin' stock and makin' you some money.' He stopped and considered and some of his enthusiasm died. 'The bad thing about it is that there's no more land in the valley with water on it. And you got to have water. I'm afraid you'll have to locate somewhere else.'

'I'll find a place. I'll start looking tomorrow.'

The meal was finished. They got up from the table and Nancy said, 'You two go out on the gallery and talk while I do the dishes.'

So Jim and Tom went out and sat in the big easy chairs and talked and smoked; and presently Nancy joined them and dusk gathered and the stars hung out their lanterns.

Payne finally said, 'Well, reckon I'll turn in. We're workin' right hard and it seems the nights ain't long enough.'

'What are you doing, Tom? Not still at calf roundup, are you?'

'No. We're prospectin' for water.'

'Water! Don't tell me the creek's quit on you.'

'No, she's still runnin' strong; but—'

He stopped, and Nancy said softly, 'Dad!'

'Yeah, Nancy; I know. But I think we

85

ought to tell Jim. It can't do no harm and he won't let it go any further.'

Jim said, 'Of course not,' and waited.

After a while Tom went on. 'It's Dave Culpepper. He's sort of hinted that he might turn the creek back into the old bed.'

Anger lifted Jim partly from the chair, but Nancy laid a hand on his arm and he settled back. 'Why should he do that?' he asked her after he had his emotions under control.

'Just pure orneriness. Soon as I heard he'd squatted on the Lazy L I rode over and talked turkey. He'd got him a tough crew, all right, and because of your brother Ed the town of Redrock was solid behind him. He told me right out that if I didn't play ball with him he'd divert the water and leave me high and dry.' Tom sighed heavily. 'I had to knuckle to him.'

'All the more reason to get the Lazy L back in a hurry.'

'Yeah. But I can't depend too much on that, son. Lately he's been makin' up to Nancy. I don't like it, and he knows it, and a showdown is due any day. If it comes to that I got to do one of two things: find another source of water or shoot him like I would a yaller dog.'

There was a short silence, then Tom went on. 'I don't want to shoot him, even if he deserves it. I've had to kill on several

86

occasions, men who were wanted for murder or worse and who knew they had nothin' to lose by shootin' it out with me. It ain't fun to kill a man, even in defense of your life. I don't want Dave's blood on my head. So me and the boys been prospectin' for water. We found some springs in the hills but not large enough to do us any good. Now we're sinkin' wells. So far we've got nothin' but dust.'

A cold anger held Jim in its grip. He had wondered at Nancy's apparent friendship for Dave; as a little girl she had always detested him. He knew now. She was playing up to him in an effort to stave off the threat to Tepee range. The anger mounted. If only he were free to deal with Dave he could order him off the Lazy L and if Dave refused to relinquish it he could shoot him as a trespasser. And have the law on his side. But not now. Not the way things stood. He would be branded a murderer, fit brother of the Kid, and hunted down like a wild beast.

Nancy said with forced cheerfulness, 'We'll find a way. Dad'll find water or you'll get the Lazy L back. I'm a good fisherman; I can play Dave for a long while. Maybe I can even tire him out.'

Tom got up. 'Sure we'll find a way. Well, I'm goin' to turn in. You'll stay the night, Jimmie.'

Jim also got up. 'No. I'm riding right now. We've got to be fishermen too, Tom. Dave can understand my calling on old friends and having supper with them, but a stay overnight would be rubbing it in. And he's mean enough to start things before we're ready for him. I'll camp on the mesa; I sort of hanker to look the old place over. If you want to get in touch with me, send Limpy. Or Nancy, if she can slip up there without tipping Dave off.'

'Maybe that's best at that,' Tom told him. 'But you're welcome here any time; you know that. Good night.'

He went into the house and for a few seconds Jim and Nancy stood on the gallery without speaking. He was aware of a feeling of new confidence; hitherto his fight had been a selfish one, calculated to profit only himself, now the welfare of the Tepee had also become an issue. He felt that he could fight the harder because of this.

He said, 'It's sure fine to have friends, isn't it, Nancy? Friends who'll stand together and fight for each other. The Lawsons and the Paynes have always been friends; for my part they always will be. Together we'll pin Dave Culpepper's ears where they belong—on the top of his head like a jackass. Good night, Nance; I'll be seein' you.'

He pressed her hand and got a warm

pressure in response.

'Good night, Jimmie. We'll catch that black stallion yet.'

It was their old customary way of parting after the wild horse had eluded them.

She walked with him to the corral, where he whistled up his bay and saddled him by starlight.

As he swung into the saddle she asked, 'You'll be at the old place?'

'Yes. You'll find me there any time after dark. So long, Nance.'

'So long, Jimmie. Be good!'

He rode off in the darkness, heading southwest towards the bulk of the mesa four miles away. His head was busy with plans. Find a good location, string some fence, bring in the cattle Nancy had saved for him. Clear the land that was needed and run up a cabin. A pole corral would do at first. Attend to his knitting and bother nobody. When the deed arrived, start action through Kling. They might delay and postpone but in the end he must win. That was it, he *must* win. For Tom and Nancy's sakes.

The mesa rose dark and forbidding before him but he did not hesitate. He circled its steep side until he came to the trail which slanted up the west wall and put his pony to it. The path was unfamiliar to the horse, but

Jimmie knew every inch of it. Guiding the nervous animal expertly, he reached the top, then cut towards the center of the rugged flat tableland where a clump of trees and brush grew about a cool spring.

At the edge of the trees he dismounted and stood for a moment making a cigarette. In the stillness he heard the sound of a dislodged stone and froze. The sound had been quite close, and he peered into the shadows beneath the trees in an effort to locate its source. He sensed rather than heard a movement behind him and whirled, dropping the cigarette and reaching for his gun.

He was too late. A dark shape struck him, sending him staggering, and a pair of muscular arms went about him. He wrestled furiously, but the surprise had been complete and he was off balance from the start. A foot tripped him and he went down heavily, the other atop him. The breath was jarred from his body, but belief that his attacker must be Dave Culpepper gave him strength and he fought back furiously.

His attacker reared back on his knees, astride of Jim, raising his gun to strike. Jim brought up an uppercut to the chin that rocked him. As he reeled back, Jim jerked a leg from beneath the fellow, doubled it and lashed out. His foot caught the other on the chest. His attacker came to his feet clear of Jim and the Colt in his hand swept down and leveled. He was in the glow of the starlight now and a certain familiarity of movement, of shape, reached Jim's consciousness just in time.

'Ed!' he gasped.

The gun jerked out of line. 'That you, Jim? Good gosh a'mighty! I come near to pluggin' you! You alone?'

'Yes.'

The Kid leaned over and helped him to his feet. The gun was back in its holster. Jim said, 'What are you doing here?'

'I might ask you the same. Come back here by the spring and we'll talk.'

They moved together into the hollow beneath the trees.

CHAPTER EIGHT

THE HOMESTEAD

The Kid built a small fire. There was no danger of its being seen for the mesa was nearly a mile wide and five hundred feet high and they were in the middle of it, in a hollow surrounded by trees.

Jim watched him broodingly. The Kid had changed in the last four years. The lithe slimness was still there, but he looked older, his actions were slower and the features had hardened into a mask that was almost cruel in its expression. The firelight deepened the lines in his cheeks and at the corners of his eyes and touched his smooth, tanned cheeks with orange. The brows met in a perpetual frown and the hazel eyes glowed like those of a mountain cougar.

The Kid got the fire burning steadily, then squatted on his heels opposite Jim and regarded him steadily. 'Now you can tell me what you're doin' on the mesa.'

'You can tell me first. It was crazy to come here, Ed. After that job in Springwater last night every man in the county's gunning for you.'

'They won't look for me here.'

'That's what you said that other night. Why did you come here?'

'Let's say I figured I might get a chance to drop in on that dance-hall gal at the Gold Standard. She sort of took my fancy. Stood right there like a soldier and held that poke out to me, and said, "I guess you'll want this." Cool as a cucumber. That's my kind of woman. Who is she?'

'Calls herself Nesta Roselle. That's all I

know about her except that she's a come-on girl at the Gold Standard. And you'd risk your neck for her!'

'I've risked it for worse.'

'What became of your gang?'

'We split up after we'd put some miles behind us. Nobody knows 'em by sight; they won't get caught. Now about you; what are you doin' here?'

Jim told him briefly, watching the eyes flare yellow in the firelight.

Ed said harshly, 'I'll settle with Dave Culpepper for you. I'll fill him so full of holes he won't hold water.'

'And what good would that do me? Think they'd let me live on the Lazy L after that? No, Ed, this is my party. You keep out of it.'

Ed shrugged and said, 'Where'd the folks move to?'

'Nearly two hundred miles west. Fifty miles north of Hartsville.'

'How's Mom?'

'Mom's dead. You killed her.'

The Kid was on his feet in one swift movement. His hand was on his gun and his eyes blazed yellow. 'Whadda you mean I killed her? I oughta plug you for that!'

Jim shrugged, eying him steadily. 'Go right ahead. If the need to kill is so deep in your blood that you'd shoot your brother, I reckon

I don't want to live anyhow. I still say you killed Mom.'

The Kid half drew the Colt, the fingers of his left hand clenching and unclenching with the fierceness of his emotion. Jim continued to regard him steadily and at last he let the weapon drop back into place, the yellow went out of his eyes, and he dropped abruptly to the ground.

'I never hurt Mom. I was good to her. I loved her.'

'You killed her, Ed. Killed her just as sure as though you had put one of your slugs into her body. Only slower.' Ed was staring at him, his lower jaw sagging just a trifle. Jim went on. 'We lived on the Lazy L and we were happy and getting along fine. Then you went bad. That was enough to kill most any mother.' He leaned forward in his earnestness. 'Can't you understand the agony of a mother who knows her son is to be hanged by the neck until dead? Knows that he's locked in a cell with guards watching to make sure he don't get away before they can spring the trap under him? Can't you understand her lyin' awake nights and grieving? Can't you?'

Ed didn't answer, but his face was tight now.

'Mom went through all that without breaking. Then they burned our home and we had to leave Redrock. There was no time to choose; we just drove what cattle we could gather in a hurry until we found a place that looked good. There were just three of us; a broken man, a woman and a seventeen-year-old kid. Mom worked right along with us. She dragged heavy logs and lifted them into place, she swung an axe, she pulled a crosscut saw. Somewhere along the line she hurt herself inwardly and got a cancer. She was in terrible pain and we couldn't do a thing for her. She got weak and thin and towards the end she couldn't get out of her bed. And at last she died. Just about a month ago. And I still say you killed her, for it wouldn't have happened if we'd been allowed to stay on the Lazy L.'

The Kid sat silent and tense on the other side of the fire watching Jim with eyes that were angry but no longer yellow. He said shortly, 'Quit preachin'. What's done is done. If I hurt Mom it was an accident. If that damned fool Tom Payne nailed in Redrock hadn't given me away nobody'd know who I was and all this wouldn't have happened. Now you told me why you came back to Redrock, but you haven't told me what brought you to the mesa tonight. I want to know.'

'Cliff Wood ordered me out of Redrock, and they don't want me in Springwater after last night. Tom Payne wanted me to stay at

95

the Tepee but it would just get people down on him. I had to camp somewhere and I figured nobody'd bother me here. Ed, you coming back and holding up that train at Junction City and then the Gold Standard right afterward sure played hob with my chances of getting the Lazy L back. Why did you do it? Why didn't you stay out of the state?'

'How the hell was I to know you was coming back? The Junction City job looked good. It was good. And I've always hated Hal Turner for the brags he's made about what he'd do to me if we met face to face.'

'It was you that shot Hal, wasn't it?'

'Sure it was me. He had no business bustin' out into the alley thataway. He'd been warned to stay put. Did I kill him?'

'He's still alive. Or was this morning. Shot through the chest.'

'I didn't see him right well when he came out. Maybe it'll teach him to listen after this.'

'Ed, I guess it's no use to ask, but I wish you'd stay out of this state. Why don't you go north or west, change your name and make a fresh start? You must have quite a pile of money laid aside.'

'Yeah, I got a nice wad, and some day I aim to retire and enjoy it. But you're talkin' foolish when you tell me to quit the owlhoot trail.

What chance would I have? I can change my name, but I can't change my height or my shape or the color of my eyes. They got reward notices posted all over the West; every lawman in the country's lookin' for me. I tell you I wouldn't have a chance. But I'll pull no more holdups in this state. That's a promise.' He got up. 'I was fixin' to leave when you came. I'll be on my way. Want to be out of the state by sunrise.'

He turned back into the trees and Jim followed him to where he had left his horse. The animal was saddled and tied. Ed tested the cinches and saw that his rifle was in the boot, then untied, got into the saddle and put out his hand. 'So long, Jim. I wish I could help you get the Lazy L back, but I'd only spoil what chances you have. I'm sorry about Mom. I did love her.'

Jim pressed the hand and let it go. Ed reined about and vanished in the shadows, heading towards the path which led through the cleft in the mesa the end of which Nancy and Jim had planned to block.

Jim stood listening until the clink of horseshoes on rock could be heard no more, then returned to the fire. He was wondering about Ed's being on the mesa, it seemed such a reckless thing to do. But then caution was not one of Ed's virtues. Perhaps he had told the truth when he said he was hanging around in the hope of finding a way to see Nesta Roselle. Some good had come from their conversation; Ed had promised to stage no more holdups in this state, and Jim knew that whatever other faults his brother might possess he was not given to lying.

He stripped his horse and picketed him on a patch of grass, then rolled in his blanket, smoked a final cigarette and slept. He rose at dawn, ate a meager breakfast, cleaned up, saddled his horse and left the mesa by the ravine in order to refresh his memory of this passage. Out on the range, he struck directly for the near-by mountain range and entered it, preferring to follow its trails rather than cross the Lazy L and risk an encounter with Dave Culpepper and his hard-bitten gang.

He knew this mountain range well, having explored it with Nancy; and as he rode there came to his mind a vague memory of a mountain park a few miles behind the Lazy L which might be the very place he was looking for. The trail he followed entered the road which led over the hills from Redrock to the town of Sage, county seat of the adjoining county, and the park lay on the south side of this road. He tried to recall the physical features of the place and the more he thought of it the more enthusiastic he became. For one thing, this mountain trail could be used when moving his cattle from the Tepee. It would be slow driving but by using this route he would not have to cross the range now controlled by Dave Culpepper.

The mesa was but a mile from Lazy L headquarters, and within a short while he knew he was directly behind its buildings, although a ridge of mountain hid them from his sight. Two hours later he came to the stream which emerged from the hills on Lazy L range. The Sage road followed the creek, and he rode through the gap through which it passed, followed it for another mile, then found himself at the edge of the park he had sought.

He drew rein and surveyed it, his eyes lighting with satisfaction. It was perfect for his plans. The road hugged the hills on this side of the creek, following the stream through another narrow gap beyond. On the far side of the stream was an expanse of lush pasture bounded by towering hills which would act as a barrier to cattle inclined to stray. Very little fence would be needed, and there was timber for his cabin, which he would build against the rimrock on the north. It remained only to be ascertained which county it was in and whether it was open to homesteading. He believed, and hoped, the land was in Sage

County; if he had to go to Springwater to file he might have trouble. He pushed ahead on the trail in the direction of Sage.

It was a forty-mile ride over mountains and through valleys on a road infrequently used, and it was late in the evening when he entered Sage. The land office was closed, so he put up at the hotel for the night and was waiting at the office when it opened the next morning. Luck was with him; the land was in Sage County and was open for settlement. He filled out his application, paid the necessary fee, and departed blithely for the town corral where he bought a second hand spring wagon and a set of harness. He hitched his horse to the wagon, drove to the hardware store to buy wire and staples and nails and the tools he would need and enough supplies to last him awhile, then set out at once on the return journey.

Traveling by wagon was slower; he camped on the trail that night and reached the homestead the following afternoon. He forded the creek, drove the wagon behind a clump of rocks where it would not be seen from the road, unhitched the horse and saddled him, and started for the mesa. He had missed two nights in succession and the Paynes might have some news for him. Certainly he had news for them!

He came out of the hills onto Lazy L range,

halted to scan the country and saw nobody, then made his way to the mesa and up the ravine to its top. He scouted and again seeing nobody, went to the hollow where Nancy or Limpy would be waiting for him if they had news. Neither had come.

He had brought some supplies with him and he cached them in a little rocky tunnel that he and Nancy had discovered, cooked a meal and ate it. He sat around until dusk, when he set out for the Tepee. He approached the house warily, not wishing to run into Dave Culpepper, and when he rode into the yard stole up to the lighted window and peered through the panes. Tom and Nancy were alone, reading. He knocked, and Nancy let him in.

'We were wondering where you were,' she told him as they went into the living room. 'Limpy rode to the mesa the night before last and again last night, but you weren't there.'

'I was in Sage,' he told them. 'I found just the place I wanted.'

He told them of the little park which he had homesteaded. Nancy remembered it well.

'Of course!' she cried. 'Why didn't we think of it before? There's grass, water, a road to Redrock and Sage, everything you need.'

'And we can drive without crossing the Lazy L. Tom, do you think you could spare

101

Limpy until I get going?'

'Sure I can. And I'll lend some boys to help drive.'

'Limpy and I can manage. It's only ten or twelve miles and we can make three or four drives of it. You need your men here.'

'I'll help you,' said Nancy. 'We can make it in two drives then.'

They talked over plans for a while, then Jim said, 'You mentioned sending Limpy over to the mesa; did you have some news for me?'

'Well, sort of. About Ed. Darn that boy, you just can't help admirin' his nerve. That night you camped on the mesa he rode into Springwater bold as you please. Syd Randall had come in with his posse right after supper. They were dog-tired and went to bed right after eatin'. Syd went into the Gold Standard for a nightcap, and just as he was comin' out, in walks Ed. He wasn't wearin' a mask but he had a gun in his hand.

'He pointed it at Syd and said, "Good evenin', Sheriff. Get your hands up and stand hitched while I 'tend to a little business. And don't nobody make a move or you'll have a new sheriff." Then he backed up against the end of the bar and looked the place over. He called to one of Hal's gals, "Come here, Nesta honey; I got somethin' for you." Wal, the gal come and stood right in front of him and said,

"What is it, Ed?" And the Kid said, "This!" and bent over and kissed her smack on the lips.

'Then, still holdin' his gun on Syd, he grinned at her and said, "That's just a sample. I'll be seein' you later, honey". Then he backed to the door, pushed outside and disappeared. Of course, Syd went tearin' after him with blood in his eye and two guns in his hands, but the Kid had circled around to the alley and Syd never did catch up with him.'

Jim said, 'I was expecting him to do something crazy like that. He was camped on the mesa when I got there and said he was hanging around in the hope of seeing one of Hal's girls who had taken his fancy. We had a talk and he promised to pull no more holdups in this state.'

'Well,' said Tom, 'I reckon you couldn't call this exactly a holdup. All he stole was a kiss.'

'He didn't steal that,' said Nancy promptly. 'From what I've heard she gave it to him— with plenty of interest.'

They talked for a while longer, then Jim went down to the bunkhouse for Limpy. The boys seemed glad to see him and their show of friendship touched him. Limpy got his gear together and saddled his horse, and they stopped at the house to say good-night. Tom said he'd have the crew haze the cattle to his northwest forty where they would be close to a trail which led into the hills, and advised Jim to be careful and not let Dave or his men see them.

'What they don't know won't hurt 'em,' he said.

They said good-night and rode swiftly to the mesa, wasting no time in conversation; but when they had made camp and were smoking their final cigarettes Limpy asked, 'You heerd about Ed's last stunt?'

'Tom told me.'

Limpy chuckled. 'I bet Syd Randall was fit to be tied. Dad-ratted youngster made a monkey of him proper. I'll be diddely-dad-burned if I wouldn't give m' eyeteeth to been there. "Come yere, Nesty!" he says, and kissed her plumb on the snoot!'

They were on Tom's northwest forty shortly after sunrise and presently saw a bunch of cattle being hazed in their direction by the Tepee crew. Jim rode to meet them. He looked the cattle over with a pleased eye, noticing their excellent condition. They were driven into a pasture and the gate was closed upon them, and after wishing Jim luck Tom and his cowboys departed to resume their search for water. Nancy had outfitted for the trail and they lost no time in getting started.

They cut out half the herd and Limpy took the point, Nancy preferring to ride the drag with Jim. There was some confusion at first, but once they were on the narrow trail they had no trouble, the animals stringing out and plodding along placidly enough.

The sun had disappeared over the hills when they arrived at the park, but when they had driven the animals across the creek Nancy had to explore it in the gathering dusk. She was as enthusiastic as Jim had been. They rode back in the darkness, separating at the mesa. Nancy refused Jim's offer of an escort; she was a range girl and not afraid of the dark, and she knew he was tired. Jim and Limpy ascended to the mesa's top, ate the supper they had postponed to this hour, and turned in at once.

The rest of the cattle were driven to the park the following day. The trip was without interruption, and Jim insisted on riding home with Nancy, leaving Limpy to make camp. When they were safely on Tepee range, Nancy made him turn back.

He rode homeward highly pleased with himself. None of his enemies knew of his homesteading venture and the cattle had been moved without attracting their attention. The coming weeks would be busy ones and he would not go near either Redrock or

Springwater. They would probably think he had been scared off, and that was just as well. He would make no move until the deed arrived; then he would ride to Springwater, have Kling get the necessary eviction order and hand it to Randall. After that it would be up to the sheriff. No matter what his personal feelings might be, he could not ignore a court order.

Jim whistled blithely as he rode.

CHAPTER NINE

ON THE BUTTON

The cattle were driven on Friday and Saturday; on Sunday Jim and Limpy started work. They went to a wooded slope a mile or so along the road and cut fence posts, trimming them and sawing them into the required lengths. When they had a sufficient number of these they ran their fence. That finished they went to work on the cabin.

The days marched by and became a week and at the end of that time they had four walls about them and a roof over their heads. Dressed lumber, glass and hardware were needed, and it was decided that Limpy should drive the wagon to Redrock and purchase them there.

When he had gone Jim rolled a cigarette and sat on a sawhorse to smoke it. The sun was low and it would be dark before Limpy got back. It was quite possible that the old fellow would linger in town for a few drinks, for it was Saturday and he had worked hard during the week.

Saturday. The second Saturday since Jim's arrival in Redrock. Tomorrow would see the end of two weeks, for he had first ridden into town on a Monday morning. He did a little mental arithmetic. He had written his father Tuesday a week ago; the letter would have gone east on Wednesday's stage. Due to poor connections it would be several days reaching Hartsville. John Lawson undoubtedly would have to return to the ranch for the old deed, then take it to Hartsville for the transfer. At the earliest the new deed would reach Redrock the following Saturday. Next Saturday night or Sunday morning he would ride to the Tepee and ascertain whether or not Tom Payne had received it.

He had not seen either Tom or Nancy all week, but she had paid them a visit while they were in the hills getting out logs, for she had left a note for him. It read, *Everything's fine. People think you left the country.*

You're doing a swell job on the cabin. Luck. Nancy. The note pleased him; his pal had not forgotten him.

So folks thought he had left the country. That was good. If they continued to think so until he had the deed, all the better. When it came he must deliver it to Newt Kling in Springwater and probably accompany him to Judge Calder's court. This he was determined to do if he had to resort to force. Syd Randall had no more right to forbid him visiting Springwater than Cliff Wood had to order him out of Redrock.

He cooked supper, busied himself with small tasks until it was dark, then went into the unfinished cabin, lighted a lantern and stretched out on a bed of boughs to read. The hours passed and Limpy did not return. He thought nothing of it at first, for the old fellow had earned a holiday; but when midnight arrived without Limpy he became uneasy. At last he went out, whistled up his bay and saddled him. He would ride towards Redrock and perhaps meet Limpy on the road.

He emerged from the mountains and skirted the edge of Lazy L range and saw the lights of Redrock. Still no Limpy. He had not met a soul, for the road was used only by the mail stages and an infrequent traveler. He continued across the valley to the edge of town, pulled off the road and squatted on his heels to smoke and wait. One o'clock came and Limpy did not appear. He got up, pinched out the cigarette and got into the saddle. He must find out what had happened to the old fellow. He rode into an alley, dismounted in the shadows of a shed and tied . . .

Inside the Pioneer saloon, Sheriff Syd Randall and Marshal Cliff Wood sat in chairs tilted against the wall talking idly and watching the throng that passed in and out. Dave Culpepper entered, stood looking about for a moment, then came over and dropped into a chair beside Cliff.

They greeted him and he said, 'What you doin' away from Springwater, Syd? The Kid might drop into the Gold Standard for another kiss.'

'He might at that, damn him! If I ever get him under my sights—!'

'Yeah, I know. But I don't think you will unless he's got his back turned. Haven't heard anything of young Lawson, have you?'

'Naw. I reckon we're rid of him.'

'Maybe he rode to Hartsville to get that deed Kling told you about.'

'I don't reckon so. I checked with Baldy Peters at the post office and he said Lawson mailed a letter to his old man Tuesday a week ago. I figure he asked the old man to send the deed to him by mail. He ain't showed up in Springwater since.'

'Ain't showed up in Redrock either,' said Cliff. 'He'd better not. I warned him out and if he shows up I'll chuck him in the calaboose.'

'Yeah?' said Dave skeptically. 'On what charge?'

'Obstructin' traffic—spittin' on the sidewalk—anything. But I'm bettin' he pulled stakes. We made it pretty plain that folks don't want no Lawsons hangin' around this neck of the woods.'

'Reckon you're right. Nancy Payne said they haven't seen him for over a week, and it seems that she'd know about it if he was still around. At the same time she'd probably know if he left. Maybe he's layin' low waitin' for that deed. What happens if he gets hold of it, Syd?'

'He takes it to Kling and Kling goes to Judge Calder and gets an order for me to put you off the Lazy L.'

'You'll play hell tryin'.'

'I can't turn down a court order, Dave. Judges are sort of touchy about the orders they issue. He'd have me kicked out of office.'

Dave said coldly, 'You come out there to put me off and you'd better fetch an army

110

with you. I'm tellin' you, Syd, I'm not givin' up that ranch to anybody. Me and the old man have sunk plenty *dinero* in the place and we aim to keep it.'

'The earliest he can get an answer to that letter is by next Saturday's stage,' Syd told him. 'That leaves you a week. If Lawson is still hangin' around your best bet is to find him and get rid of him before next Saturday.'

'Where would he be hidin' out?' asked Cliff. 'He got to eat; he'd have to buy supplies somewhere.'

'There's Sage,' said Dave tightly. 'He might go over there.'

Randall's eyes narrowed. 'Yeah. Also he might have told his old man to mail the deed there. Dave, it looks kinda bad for you.'

'Me, I think he's lit out,' said Cliff. 'He oughta have sense enough to know that even if he got the Lazy L back, folks wouldn't let him live on it.'

They sat in silence for a minute or so, Dave gazing frowningly across the room. Finally he snapped out of his reverie, got up abruptly and said, 'Let's have a drink.'

They were about to cross to the bar when the back door opened and Bud Falk came in. Bud owned a saloon farther up the street. He was short and stout and bald, and Art Fenton, the bank cashier whom the Kid had shot, had been his wife's brother. Consequently he hated all Lawsons. He glanced about, saw them and crossed the floor to where they stood. He said in a low voice, 'Jim Lawson's still around.'

They stiffened. 'Where?' asked Dave sharply.

'That I don't know. Listen. You know old Limpy that works for Payne? Well, he came into my place and joined up with three of the Tepee boys at the bar. They asked him how he liked his new job and of course I pricked up my ears. Didn't know he'd got a new job; figured he was a fixture on the Tepee same as a corral post. Limpy said that he liked it except that him and Jim had been working like a pair of beavers stringing fence and running up a cabin. Get it? Him and *Jim*.'

'Lots of fellers named Jim,' said Cliff.

'Sure. But how many of them would Limpy be helping string fence and building a cabin?'

'Bud's right,' said Syd emphatically. 'It's Lawson he's helpin'. I know 'em both from 'way back. Limpy taught young Lawson how to ride and rope. They used to be thick as thieves.'

'Where are they doin' all this work?' asked Dave.

'Don't know. I listened until they broke up but Limpy didn't say. When the other boys left I came right over. Limpy was still at the bar.'

'Get him,' said Dave to Randall. 'Find out where Lawson's hidin' out.'

'Not me,' said Syd hastily. 'I ain't foolin' with Limpy. Everybody likes him and election's this fall. If it was young Lawson—'

'I'll handle it,' said Cliff, 'I'll get it out of the old coot. He don't like me and I don't like him. Leave it to me.'

He started for the front door and Bud Falk left by the rear one. Dave and Syd walked over to the bar. He moved to a window through which he could watch the old man and stood there in the shadows. He saw Limpy buy another drink, then look at an old silver watch and start for the door. Cliff waited until he had come out, then drew his Colt, stepped close to Limpy and nudged him in the side with it.

'Keep walkin', Limpy. Right down to my office. I want to talk to you.'

Limpy halted, stiffened, then relaxed. Resistance would get him nothing but a bullet and if Cliff Wood thought he could get anything out of him he had another think coming. He started walking, the gun nudging him. Cliff took him by an arm.

'Git your dad-ratted dirty fingers off'n me!' snapped Limpy.

113

Cliff released the arm.

They crossed the street and went into Cliff's office. There was a lamp, wick turned low, burning on the desk. Limpy would have stopped there but Cliff said, 'Right on back, Limpy. We don't want to be interrupted.'

Limpy went back into the jail corridor. There were four cells and they were all empty, their doors hanging wide. Cliff had picked up the lamp; he pulled the corridor door shut and motioned Limpy into a cell.

'You dad-ratted son of a mangy polecat!' said Limpy hotly. 'You can't arrest me!'

'I ain't arrestin' you; I just want to talk to you. Get inside.'

Old Limpy glared at him, spat, and went into the cell. Cliff put the lamp on the floor and followed him. He took Limpy's gun and tossed it outside the cell, then drew out a blackjack. He faced Limpy, balancing it in his hand.

'I want to know where Jim Lawson's hangin' out.'

'You go plumb to hell!'

'Maybe this'll jog your memory.'

Cliff hit him with the blackjack . . .

*   *   *

The streets were very dark. Jim pulled his hat

low over his eyes and stepped from the passageway where he had been standing. Saturday night noise droned in his ears, muted but continuous. He could see occasional shapes as men moved into little areas of illumination on their way from place to place.

He walked along the street, circling wide to avoid what dim light seeped through grimy windows or over half-doors. When he came to a saloon he moved to a window or a position where he could look over the doors, scanning the interior for a sight of Limpy. He saw Dave Culpepper and Syd Randall in the Pioneer and wondered why Cliff Wood wasn't with them. He didn't see Limpy in any of the places.

His wagon, loaded, stood at the hitching rail ouside Jeb Culpepper's store, the horse, humped on three legs, alseep. He ventured up on the steps and looked inside. Limpy was not there. Nor was Cliff Wood. Dissatisfied, he made another circuit of the town, checking for both Limpy and Cliff. He could not locate either. He slipped into a passageway and rolled and lighted a cigarette. He had investigated every open business place in town and had not seen either Limpy or Cliff. The simultaneous absence of both was not pure coincidence. He took a long drag on the cigarette, stamped it beneath his boot, clamped his jaws tight and walked to the marshal's office.

It was dark. He tried the door and found it unlocked. Softly he opened it and stepped inside. There was a faint crack of light showing beneath the door to the corridor. The noise of the town filtered through the doorway; he closed the door. He heard a thud, a groan, then a low tense voice saying, 'Where is he? Talk, damn you! Where is he?'

Jim drew his Colt, stepped lightly to the corridor door and pulled it open. There was a lamp on the floor and it dimly illuminated the first cell on his left. In the corner of that cell he could see the bulk of a man with his back turned. He was bending over another man crumpled in the corner and he held a blackjack in his hand.

Cliff Wood said, 'Tell me, damn you! Loosen up or I'll hand you another. Just a little tap, Limpy, to loosen your tongue.'

'Go—hell—yuh dad-ratted—!'

The blackjack came up. Jim said, 'Hold it, Cliff!'

The blackjack remained in the air as Cliff Wood slowly straightened. He turned his head carefully and Jim saw a sagging jaw and a pair of startled eyes. The man on the floor had gone limp.

Jim walked into the cell, face tight and eyes

116

burning. He walked like a cougar quickly, lightly. He stopped behind Cliff Wood with his gun against the marshal's back. He jerked Cliff's Colt out of its holster and sent it spinning through the cell doorway; he snatched the blackjack and tossed it after the gun. Then he holstered his own Colt and took Cliff by the shoulder and spun him around.

Cliff raised the other hand. He said, 'Take it easy, Jim! I was just—'

Jim hit him on the button with everything he had. The pain of contact went through his knuckles and into his wrist and along his arm clear to the shoulder. Cliff was knocked back against the stone wall; he bounced off and wilted, unconscious before he hit the ground.

Jim bent over Limpy, raised the sagging head. Limpy was out. There were bruises on his face and blood seeped slowly from cuts on his cheeks. Jim picked the old man up in his arms, carried him outside into the corridor and propped him against the wall. He got Limpy's gun and put it in Limpy's holster, then went into the front office and got the jail keys from the nail on the wall. He went back, closed the cell door on the unconscious marshal and locked it. He tossed the keys into a corner, picked up Limpy and went out into the office, kicking the door shut behind him.

He opened the front door, waited until the

117

coast was clear, then carried the old man into the passageway beside the jail. He left him in the alley, got his horse and rode to the store. He tied his horse to the tail gate, untied the one in the shafts and climbed up on the seat. He was not trying to keep out of sight; if Syd or Dave happened to see him there would be a shoot-out and perhaps another Lawson would be branded a killer.

Nobody noticed him. He drove to the first intersection, then turned into the alley. Limpy was still unconscious when he loaded him into the wagon. He set out for the homestead.

CHAPTER TEN

IN THE NIGHT

Dave Culpepper and Syd Randall found Cliff an hour later. Impatient at his failure to return, they set out in search of him, but since nobody had seen him take Limpy to the jail that was the last place they looked. Cliff was shaking the cell bars and swearing with great fervor.

'This finishes it,' he declared when they had released him. 'I got Lawson right where I want him now. Attackin' an officer in the performance of his duty, assault with intent to kill—the works! By Judas, I'll have him sent up for so long he'll have white whiskers when he gets out!'

'What about Limpy?' asked Dave. 'He'll appear for Lawson.'

'The hell with Limpy! He was out when me and Lawson tangled, and it'll be my word against Lawson's. Don't you worry. Don't you worry one bit. I'll get Jim Lawson and get him good.'

'All we got to do now is locate him. I'll get my boys on the job tomorrow mornin'!'

'And I'll ride with 'em. And I only hope that he puts up a fight when we find him. If he does I'll fix him so's the only deed he'll need is one to a three-by-six lot!'

They had a drink on it, Dave and Syd left him after agreeing to meet at Dave's ranch early on Sunday morning...

Limpy recovered consciousness before the wagon had gone very far and climbed over to the seat beside Jim. He was smoldering with anger.

'The dad-ratted son of a misbegot vinegaroon! Thought he could make me talk. Batted me around with a blackjack, the dad-ratted mangy son of a polluted polecat! He's gonna pay for that, youbetcha! What did yuh do to the skunk?'

'Nearly busted my arm bouncing him off the wall. He was out cold when we left and I locked him in the cell. Limpy, this means war. They're going to find out where we are and then come after us.'

'Let 'em come! That park was made to order, and we built the cabin back in a corner against that rimrock where they can't get at us except from the creek. I'm a man of peace, but I'll be diddely-dad-burned if anybody's gonna slam me around with a blackjack and git away with it! Let 'em come; we'll pepper hell outa them.'

They wasted no time in preparing for eventualities. When they reached the homestead Jim filled a keg with water and hauled it to the cabin, and they worked the rest of the night fortifying the place. They carried the lumber and supplies into the house, sawed some planks to length and nailed them over the windows, leaving cracks between them wide enough to admit their rifle barrels. Thanks to Limpy's purchases of that evening they had enough supplies.

When dawn came they cooked and ate breakfast and Jim made Limpy lie down for a few hours' sleep. When he had washed up the dishes Jim rolled a cigarette and sat on a sawhorse to smoke it, his rifle close at hand.

He gazed about the park looking for a possible means of approach other than from the creek. On the far side was a break in the rimrock which led to a ravine-like passageway between two lines of hills and eventually ended in a box canyon a few miles to the northwest. Not much likelihood of an approach from that direction. Jim decided that if an attack came it must be from the road beyond the creek.

After three hours' rest Limpy awakened and Jim slept. When he awoke the smell of wood smoke and coffee was in the air. They ate dinner, cleaned up, then sat around watching and waiting. Two hours later a single rider came into view, moving at a trail lope towards Sage. He pulled up and they could see his face as he looked towards them, but the distance was too great for identification. He moved on and disappeared beyond the shoulder of hill.

Limpy said, 'I ain't sure, but that hoss looked like one from the Circle C. If I could see his other flank I'd know. Got a white patch on the shoulder.'

'That settles it,' said Limpy. 'Circle C hairpin. We been spotted. The dad-ratted varmints'll be ridin' our way. I only hope that lousy son of a lop-eared coyote of a Cliff Wood's with 'em.'

They waited another hour, then once more

121

a single rider came into view. This time there was no doubt of the person's identity.

'It's Nancy,' said Limpy. 'Dang it, she would show up in time to spoil a good fight!'

Jim went to meet her. She slipped from her pony and smiled at him.

'Nice work, cowboy! Looks real homelike.' She indicated the rifles with a wave of her hand. 'Expecting an attack by Indians?'

'Not Injuns,' said Limpy. 'Polecats. A whole passel of 'em. And we don't aim to git smelled up, neither.'

Jim answered the question in her face. 'Had a run-in with Cliff Wood last night and about an hour ago one of Dave's riders spotted us. They know where we are now and we're expecting a visit.'

Her face went sober. 'Then I'll wait.' She dropped the rein and sat on the sawhorse Jim had vacated.

'I wish you wouldn't.' He knew her idea in remaining. Cliff Wood and company would be reluctant to start anything in the presence of a witness. The trouble was that Dave would undoubtedly be with Cliff. 'There's that fish you're playing, you know.'

'I don't care. I'm getting tired of playing that fish. Dave usually comes over to take me riding right after dinner, but he didn't show up today. I'll just tell him that I waited an

122

hour then decided to ride alone. I noticed the park and wondered—and found you. Nothing wrong with that, is there?'

'Not that I can see. But Dave's different.'

She shrugged. 'There's a limit to the patience of even a fisherman.'

Limpy grabbed his rifle and stood up. 'Here they come!'

Jim said sharply, 'No shooting. Let me handle this.'

A band of horsemen had come into view from behind the hill. One of them leaned from his saddle and snipped the wire, and the whole bunch rode through the gap and forded the creek. They came on at a gallop, fanning out into a thin line.

Jim stood by the sawhorse watching, his rifle still leaning against a stack of lumber. Limpy said, 'Dad-rat it, Jim! Git your rifle.'

'Take it easy. Don't make a threatening move. Let me handle it.'

There were nine of them: Dave and his six hard-bitten punchers, Cliff Wood and Syd Randall. They came on swiftly until they recognized Nancy, then Cliff raised a hand and they pulled down to a trot. A hundred feet away from the little group and the trot became a walk. They drew closer together.

Cliff Wood and Syd Randall were in front, and Cliff was scowling at Jim. When they were ten feet away Jim said, 'I reckon that's close enough.'

They halted and Cliff Wood got from his horse and came forward. Jim made no move except to clinch his right fist suggestively. 'I said that's far enough, Cliff.'

Cliff stopped. 'You're under arrest,' he said shortly.

'I told you once your authority was limited to the town of Redrock.'

'So you did. So we'll make it real nice and legal.' He turned to Syd Randall. 'You tell him, Syd.'

Rendall got off his horse and came forward purposefully. 'I'm arrestin' you, Jim Lawson, for interferin' with an officer in the performance of his duty and for assault with intent to kill.'

'You can't arrest me any more than Cliff can, Syd.'

'Since when? I'm sheriff of Redrock County, ain't I?'

'Sure you are. But this happens to be Sage County.'

That jarred Randall. He looked startled, but recovered quickly. 'You can't pull no bluff like that on me, Lawson. You come along with me.'

'No can do,' said Jim mildly. 'I tell you this homestead's in Sage County. I had to look it up when I filed, you know. And I had to file at Sage. The dividing line follows the base of those hills. Right now you're trespassing on private property. My property.'

Syd glanced at Cliff and Cliff returned the glance; then they both turned to look at Dave Culpepper. For once Dave had no suggestion to offer. He was scowling at Nancy, his anger directing itself at the girl. If she weren't present they could go ahead with their plans regardless of the county line; as it was, there was nothing to do but admit defeat, even if that defeat were only temporary.

He growled, 'What're you doin' here. Nancy?'

She smiled at him. 'You had a date to ride with me but didn't show up, so I started out alone. I came here.'

'You knew he was here all the time!'

'I was sure I could find him. He wouldn't have taken those Lazy L cows we'd been keeping for him if he hadn't a place to take them, would he?'

'You didn't tell me.'

'You didn't ask me.'

'You said you hadn't seen him for a week.'

'That's right. The last time I saw him was a week ago yesterday.'

For another few seconds Dave continued to glare at her, then he said shortly, 'Let's go,'

125

and wheeled his horse. His men followed him away at a smart lope.

Cliff Wood was very red in the face. His jaws were clamped tightly and he appeared as though he might explode at any moment. He glared at Jim and then at Limpy and finally he found words.

'This ain't the end of this business by no means. I'll get the pair of you before I'm through or eat my hat—and like it.'

'Then yuh better git ready to chaw,' Limpy told him fiercely. 'And don't ask for no salt, neither. Now git outa here. And splice that wire yuh cut when you're through it.'

Syd Randall turned back to his horse saying, 'Come on, Cliff,' and Cliff, after a few more futile glares, followed him. They rode away slowly, and it appeared that Randall was arguing with his brother officer. They did not splice the wire.

Nancy said, 'Now suppose you tell me what happened last night.'

Limpy told her, finding some difficulty in restraining his language.

She was indignant. 'That's the rottenest thing I ever heard of! Beating an old man with a blackjack to make him talk!'

'Who's old?' yelled Limpy. 'If I can't take that dad-ratted Cliff Wood apart any day of the week, fifty-two weeks to the year, I'll be a diddely-dad-burned son of a lop-eared rhinoceros!'

'Sure, sure,' soothed Jim. 'Cliff knows it too, or he wouldn't have bothered to get the drop on you last night. But we've got to play sort of foxy. We've got to figure out what Syd and Cliff'll try next.'

'What *can* they try?' Nancy wanted to know.

'Well, if I was guilty, and if they really wanted me, Syd'd go to the sheriff at Sage and ask for my arrest. I think the best bet is to beat him to it and tell our story first.'

'Then we'd better be startin' before daylight,' said Limpy. 'It's all of forty miles to Sage.'

'You can't both go,' said Nancy. 'You can't leave the place unguarded.'

'We'll have to risk it. My word alone won't count against Randall's; but if Limpy is there to back it up I think we can copper Syd's bet.'

'I could get Dad to send a couple of our boys over.'

'Don't do it. You two are in deep enough now. Have you found water yet?'

'No. But we will. We just got to! And, Jim, I meant to tell you, your deed didn't come on yesterday's stage.'

'The earliest we can expect it is next Saturday. It should be here then.'

She left them shortly thereafter and they agreed to spell each other at watching during the night, although Jim was sure there would be no attack as long as the chance of removing him through legal channels remained.

The night passed uneventfully and they started on their journey before dawn. They reached Sage around one in the afternoon and found the sheriff in his office at the courthouse. Jim introduced himself and Limpy and told his story frankly, and Sheriff Trotter seemed impressed. When Limpy told of his beating at the hands of Cliff Wood, Trotter made his decision.

'I'm glad you men came to me at once. I don't know Randall very well and he would have talked me into ordering your arrest. In fact, with only his charges to go on I wouldn't have had any choice in the matter. Now it's different.' He puckered his forehead in thought for a short space, then said, 'You boys get your horses off the street, then come back here. You can wait in the next office and hear what Randall says if he comes.'

They put their horses up and went back to the sheriff's office, entered the adjoining room and left the door slightly ajar. They found a deck of cards and started a game of casino. An hour passed, two hours; then they heard a voice say, 'Sheriff Trotter? I'm Sheriff

Randall from Redrock County. I want you to arrest a feller that's crossed the line into your jurisdiction.'

'Glad to co-operate where co-operation's called for, Randall. Who is it you want and what do you want him for?'

'Feller named Jim Lawson. Heard of the Kid, ain't you? Well, his name is Ed Lawson and this is his brother. And he's beginnin' to shape up just like the Kid. He sneaked into the Redrock jail while the marshal was questionin' a feller that works for him, danged near kills the marshal and gets away with the prisoner. He's got a homestead just over the line and when I went out there yesterday after him, he defied me to touch him. Of course, I couldn't, him bein' in your county. Just send a deputy along with me and we can handle it easy.'

'You got a witness to this assault on the marshal, I reckon?'

'You never mind the witness; we'll take care of that end. You just arrest this Jim Lawson and turn him over to me. I'll see that he's convicted.'

'Yes, I reckon you would. Well, Randall, I'll not arrest him.'

'You won't—! Damn it, man, you gotta!'

'I don't think so. You see, I've heard the other side of the story.' He raised his voice.

'Come on in, Lawson!'

Jim and Limpy stepped into the other room, and at the sight of them Randall's jaw went slack and he instinctively reached for his gun.

'Don't try it, Randall,' said Sheriff Trotter coldly. 'These men have told me their story and I believe it. They live in my county and I'll not see citizens of Sage framed. Do you want to hear the story they told me?'

Randall didn't. He shifted from one foot to the other, frowning alternately at Jim and Limpy and Sheriff Trotter. Finally he exploded with a violent 'Damn!' and bolted from the room.

'If I were you,' advised Trotter, 'I'd sort of keep my eyes open on the way back.'

They said they would, thanked him warmly and went out. Randall had already mounted his horse and was heading for Redrock:

'Be midnight before he gits home,' remarked Limpy. 'And that goes for us too.'

Jim glanced quickly at the old man. The ride had wearied Limpy but he was game for a return trip without rest. It was Jim's opinion that eighty hard miles at a stretch was beyond the old fellow's strength. Still it was necessary that they get back at once to protect their property. He said casually, 'Why don't you lay over here for the night, Limpy, and ride to

130

the homestead tomorrow? I can hold the fort until you get there.'

'Think I'm a weaklin'?' snapped Limpy. 'I'm as good in the saddle as you any day. And there oughta be two to hold that place. I'll be diddely-dad-burned if yuh leave me behind!'

So they ate a combined dinner and supper and started back. Jim tried to take it easy but Limpy wouldn't have it that way. He kept urging Jim to greater speed, swearing that he could maintain any pace that Jim could set; and all the while his face grew tighter, his eyes duller. With the coming of darkness Limpy began to lag; he'd slacken his vigilance, the tired horse would immediately drop to a walk, then Limpy would come alive briefly and once more force the pace.

The end came at last. Jim, not hearing the beat of hoofs behind him, turned back. He found Limpy's horse standing with lowered head on the trail and Limpy dazedly, futilely, trying to pull himself into the saddle. The old man was cursing himself for a weakling but the oaths could not spur him to greater effort.

Jim said, 'This settles it, old-timer; we're going to camp right here.'

'Gotta go on! Yuh dad-ratted—son of a— locoed jughaid! We gotta—'

Jim pulled him away from the horse. 'Come on; I'm dead beat and so the horses. We're

131

going to camp.'

He led the old man, staggering with weariness, to one side of the trail and made him sit down. Limpy promptly fell on his back. Jim off-saddled the horses and staked them out, then built a fire.

Limpy opened dull eyes. 'You go—ahead, Jim. I'll rest—a mite—and then ketch up with yuh.' His eyes closed again and he was asleep.

Jim sat by the campfire smoking and thinking. He couldn't leave Limpy here; the old man was game to the core, but he might be so stiff and sore by morning that he would be unable to saddle up and get on his horse. They had brought no blankets; he finally curled up close to the fire and slept.

Several times during the night he awoke to replenish the fire. When he awoke at dawn it was to see Limpy painfully hobbling about trying to regain the use of his limbs. Jim saddled up and helped him onto his horse and they started out again. Despite Limpy's protest he held to a walk. It was midmorning when they rounded the shoulder of hill and could look into the park. It was as he had feared.

The fence was down, torn up post by post, and rolled into an inextricable mass. Where the cabin had stood was a bed of ashes and embers from which arose a thin column of blue smoke. And there wasn't a head of cattle in sight.

CHAPTER ELEVEN

THE LOVE OF NESTA

They sat their saddles in silence for a full three minutes, gazing with dead eyes on the scene of ruin, too discouraged to speak. Even Limpy's vocabulary failed him. Presently Jim nudged his horse with a heel and they moved dejectedly to the ford, crossed it and rode to the cabin.

Everything was gone but the wagon. The lumber had been carried inside and had been stored there with all their supplies. There wasn't a thing remaining to satisfy their appetites if they had had any. Their blankets were gone and all their spare equipment.

Jim's thoughts were bitter ones. He had leaned backward to avoid trouble; the two blows he had struck had been defensive ones. He had knocked Dave down when Dave had attacked him; he had hit Cliff Wood only after the marshal had tortured Limpy.

He remembered the words of Nesta Roselle: 'They'll pick on you and hurt you

133

every way they can and finally you'll go on the prod and they'll say you're just as bad as your brother.' Certainly at that moment he felt like going on the prod. He felt like riding to the Circle C, walking up to Dave in the midst of his men and shooting him in his tracks. He felt at the moment that he could get away with it. And then he would ride into Redrock and do the same to Cliff Wood. And Syd Randall, if he took a hand. There was no fear of consequences; if they outlawed him he'd side with Ed and fight society with every bit of brain and brawn that he possessed. They had driven him to it. He had tried to get a square deal and they had denied him it.

And then he thought of Nancy, of Tom Payne, of Sheriff Trotter. They had given him breaks; bigger breaks than he had deserved. He couldn't let them down; more to the point, he couldn't let himself down. He had come back with a determination that had been formed over a period of four hard years; he had steeled himself against ridicule, animosity, hatred. To go on a wild rampage now would be to defeat that determination, would give them the very weapon they wanted: the chance to say I told you so.

He expelled his breath and eased himself in the saddle. He got out tobacco and papers and started rolling a cigarette.

Limpy said miserably, 'It's all my fault. I'm a dad-ratted weaklin'—a throwed-away old man.'

Jim turned his head slightly and saw two big tears roll down the leathery cheeks, and quickly looked away again.

He said, 'It wasn't your fault, Limpy. It wasn't my fault. It was just in the cards that they wouldn't let us stay here in peace. Sooner or later they'd have found a way to do it; in the night, perhaps. Or after they had drawn us away on some wild-goose chase. But if they think they have us licked they're mighty mistaken. That deed should be here Saturday, and then I'm riding to Springwater with it if I have to shoot my way to Newt Kling's office and from there to Judge Calder's court. Dave Culpepper has destroyed our home; we'll take that nice house he's built in exchange and make him like it.'

'By grab! I wanta be on hand when you do it! I wanta help kick him off'n the Lazy L. The dad-ratted lousy son of a dad-ratted—' He broke off suddenly. 'Jim, let's go back to Sage. Let's get Sheriff Trotter after 'em. It's in his county; he can give 'em the works.'

'Not a chance, Limpy. This place is in his county, but they're in Redrock. Think Syd Randall's going to turn his friends over to Trotter? Not by a jugful; especially since

Trotter refused to turn us over to him.'

'But they rustled our stock. That's a hangin' offense!'

'I don't believe they rustled them. Syd Randall couldn't afford to be a party to that. They probably drove them into the valley. Let them stay there for the time being. Dave Culpepper can't very well change a Lazy L to a Circle C.'

'But what're we goin' to do?'

Jim smoked thoughtfully for a short while. At last he said, 'We're going to stay right here and run up another shelter of some sort. Nothing fancy. Then we're going to post trespassing signs all over the place and make them stick. With rifles, if necessary.'

'What do we do about grub and blankets?'

'We'll ride over to the Tepee and get a handout from Tom; then you'll stay here and I'll drive the wagon to Sage and load up.'

Limpy thrust out his chin. His night's rest had restored some of his strength and all of his belligerency, and Jim's courage had but added to his own determination. 'I'm with you every jump in the trail until I fall offn' my hoss; and the next time I do that you ride on and leave me. We'll go over to the Tepee and fill our bellies, then while you're drivin' to Sage I'll whittle out some trespassin' signs and stick 'em around the place and the first person that steps on our property that hadn't oughta is gonna git welcomed with a .44-calibre kiss.'

They rode to the Tepee and Nancy fed them and outfitted them with a couple of blankets apiece and enough food to last for several days. They returned to the homestead and camped for the night, Jim postponing the trip to Sage until the next day in order to rest his horse. They found some boards and printed NO TRESPASSING signs with charcoal, of which there was a plentiful supply. These were nailed to fence posts salvaged from the wreck and planted at intervals along the creek. They slept beneath the wagon that night, and early the following morning Jim hitched up and started for Sage. He left Limpy sitting determinedly on the sawhorse, his rifle in his hands and homicide in his heart . . .

Wednesday night was a dull night at the Gold Standard. There were a few regulars at the bar, but the games were for the most part idle, with a couple of miners desultorily shooting craps, the faro dealer playing solitaire and the roulette dealer practicing putting the ball into number 28.

Nesta Roselle sat at a table in the corner idly fingering an empty whiskey glass. It was the same table at which she had sat with young Jimmie Lawson, but it was not Jim of whom she was thinking. She was thinking of his brother Ed. He whom they called the Kid. She had thought of him quite often since the night he had held Syd Randall at bay with a Colt while he kissed her.

That kiss had done something to Nesta. She was as used to kisses as a politician is used to handshakes, but this one had been different. Her lips still tingled with the sweetness of it; it had reawakened girlhood dreams that had been forgotten in a world of somewhat sordid realities. Nesta found herself longing to see the Kid again.

Had it not been for the wall beside her she might have done so. Beyond the wall was a dark, narrow passageway which led to the alley, and standing in the mouth of that passageway was the Kid. He too had remembered that kiss, and had dared much to see Nesta again.

He waited with the patience which had become a habit for the appearance of one of two men or both of them. They must be taken care of before he could risk a call on Nesta. Syd Randall would shoot him on sight and so would Ed Hall, once his guard and now Marshal of Springwater. Hal Turner was still in bed—or should be—recovering from the wound the Kid had inflicted. The others didn't count; his reputation was such that he knew he could ride down the main street in broad daylight and nobody would even dare say *Boo*! He grinned sardonically at the thought.

Boots thudded on the board sidewalk and the Kid tensed. A man walked to the half-doors of the Gold Standard and stood looking over them. The light from within illuminated his face. He was Ed Hall, the marshal.

He stood looking into the saloon for the space of ten heartbeats, then turned and continued his course down the sidewalk. And as he passed the slit between the two buildings the Kid stepped out beside him and the Kid's right arm went about him and his hand closed firmly on the butt of the Colt which swung at Ed Hall's right hip.

Ed stopped abruptly, half turning, his hand going to where his gun should have been. It was there no longer. It was nudging him in the back and the Kid was saying, 'Easy, Ed. Keep walkin'. Let's make this friendly, huh?'

Hall gasped, 'Kid!' and started walking again.

The Kid took Ed's arm and turned him into the next passageway and through it into the alley. He asked, 'Where's Randall?'

'I d-don't know. R-Redrock, I reckon.'

The Kid frowned. Why was it that supposedly hard men got chicken-hearted and stammery when they talked to him? Hall was acting just as he had four years before when the Kid had covered him as he stood on the bunk.

'Listen, Ed,' he said gruffly. 'I ain't goin' to hurt you. I ain't even goin' to hold up anybody in your stinkin' town. You say Randall's in Redrock?'

Hall spoke more confidently. 'Far as I know, Kid.'

They crossed the alley to a barn and the Kid halted Ed at its entrance and felt him over for weapons. There was a knife and he took it. He said, 'Cross your wrists behind you, Ed.'

He tied the wrists with a length of rope and pushed Ed into the barn. He urged him forward to a small room where feed was kept. Inside this he said, 'Want to stand up or lay down?'

'Lay down,' said Ed and obligingly stretched out on the floor.

The Kid tied the end of the rope to a post, then bound Ed's ankles.

'Guess I'll have to gag you, Ed. Like old times, huh?'

Ed did not answer. The Kid took Ed's scarf from around his neck and made a gag of it, trying the ends behind Ed's head. He said, 'Maybe you can work loose, but I wouldn't try it for an hour or so.'

He went out and shut the door behind him,

140

crossed the alley and went up the passageway to the street, then walked along it to the Gold Standard. He pulled his hat low over his eyes and walked to the entrance and looked over the top of the doors. One bartender was polishing glasses, the other was leaning over the bar conversing with two earnest and inebriated customers. Two miners were shooting craps, the faro dealer was playing solitaire, the roulette man was whirling the wheel and tossing the ball. The Kid turned his head to the right and saw Nesta at the corner table. He grinned and pushed through the doors and walked swiftly towards her. Nobody had heard him enter and nobody paid him any attention.

He circled softly behind her chair and stood close to the wall. He said, 'Hello, honey.'

Nesta snapped out of her reverie and looked up quickly. Her eyes went round and her lips parted and she raised one hand to her breast. He shook his head and laid a finger on his lips. She closed her mouth and the surprise went out of her face and she glanced quickly about the room.

He leaned over and kissed her shining hair, then dropped into a chair and said, 'Tell that barkeep to fetch a couple whiskeys, honey.'

Her hand came out to grip his arm. 'Ed! Ed, you daren't! They'll kill you!'

'They won't unless you turn sissy on me. Order those whiskeys, hon.'

Nesta waited until he had lowered his head, then called across the room. 'Pete! A couple of ryes!'

The bartender who was talking with the two customers jerked erect, threw a glance at their table, saw a customer and said, 'Comin' up!' When he reached the table the customer had his head bent over a roll of bills. He detached one and tossed it on the table without looking up. 'Keep the change,' he said, and the bartender said, 'Thanks, Bud,' and returned to the bar.

It was gloomy in the corner and Nesta hitched her chair so that she was between Ed and the bar. She leaned over the table and he kissed her. She said, 'Ed, you're taking an awful risk!'

He laughed deep in his throat. 'It's worth it, hon. I've waited a long while for this. Listen hon; let's get away from this. You and me together! I got a nice little stake laid away and I can get more. We'll go down to Mexico— South America—Europe, even. How about it, hon?'

His eyes shone and he had clasped her hands tightly in his eagerness.

She gasped, 'Ed! Now?'

'Right now! You wait right here; I'll get a

hoss—'

'Ed! Oh, Ed, I—I don't know—'

'Listen, honey! I know it's sudden. I know it's crazy. But we ain't like other folks. We ain't got the time to court and flirt and be coy. This might be the last time I'd get to see you. And I'm crazy about you. I lay awake nights thinkin' of you.' He was squeezing her hands so tightly it hurt but she was not aware of the pain. 'What is there here for you? Nothin' but a lot of dirty work among a lot of dirty drunks, bein' pawed over by a bunch of skunks you'd like to spit on! All for a few lousy dollars that there's no place to spend noway. Ah, Nesta, honey, come with me! Tonight—now!'

She stared at him, fascinated, moved to her very soul. He did love her; she was wise enough in the ways of man to know truth when she saw it. And it came to her with the suddenness of a ray of sunlight through cloud that she loved him, too. Deeply, honestly.

She turned her hands and gripped both of his, hard. 'I'll do it, Ed! Just give me time to get a few things. I'll be right down, darling.'

Somehow they found themselves on their feet. He put his arms around her and held her very close. She yielded her body, raised her lips. And with the kiss she gave him her life, her soul.

The bartender was staring. So were the two

143

customers. They paid no attention. The Kid put her from him reluctantly. 'Hurry, honey! I'll get a hoss.'

He strode straight to the doorway, his hat back, his face transfigured. He strode rapidly along the street, his customary caution gone. His head was among the stars. He had thought to steal the first good horse he came upon, but now he could not bring himself to do this. He hurried to the livery corral.

The liveryman knew him and was paralyzed with fright. He was surprised when the Kid asked him the price of his best horse and rig. The Kid paid for both with gold and led the saddled animal away. He went straight to the Gold Standard, aflame to see Nesta again, not content until they were over the state line and in a safe place.

He did not notice the horse which stood at the hitching rack, a horse that he knew well. The glance that he sent over the half doors was a cursory one; he saw only Nesta. She had put a cloak over her evening gown and there was a cute little poke bonnet perched on her golden curls. She was watching the door with wide, anxious eyes and her face was tense and strained. But that, he thought, would be because of the excitement.

He pushed through the doors and took two long strides towards her.

Syd Randall's voice said, 'This time I got you, Kid!'

He whirled, but for once he was too late. Randall had risen from behind the bar and his Colt was aimed at the Kid's chest. There was no hope and the Kid knew it, but he must make the try. His hand flashed downward. He heard Nesta scream, '*Ed!*'

She leaped forward, her arms extended. They went about his neck and her slim body swung in front of him. Randall fired and somebody cried, 'God A'mighty!'

The Kid felt the spasmodic jerk of her body when the bullet struck it, and at the same time he felt the heart within him split as though under the impact of the same slug. His gun was out of its holster; he raised it and fired and if he had ever shot to kill it was now. The bullet struck Randall squarely between the eyes and he was dead before he hit the floor.

The Kid put both arms about Nesta and hugged her close. Her head was tilted back and her eyes were open and staring. He laid his cheek against hers and sobbed, 'Nesta, my darlin'! Oh, my darlin'!'

The silence of death was in the room. Nobody glanced towards the bar behind which Syd Randall lay. They were watching the Kid, and in that tragic moment not one of them remembered that he was the Kid. He was just a boy who had lost something more precious than life itself.

Afterwards men wondered at their own behavior. Here was a killer with a reward on his head, his defenses down, vulnerable. But nobody made a move to seize him. They just stood and watched. Somebody took the smoking gun out of his hand, but when they would have taken Nesta from him he turned on them savagely.

'Get your hands off her! She's mine! Nobody'll take her from me!'

He stood there holding her dead weight for quite a while, sobbing into the yellow curls that tumbled from beneath the poke bonnet; then, as though just recovering consciousness, he raised his head and looked dazedly about him. He saw the man with the gun in his hand and reached out and the man gave it to him. He holstered the weapon, put his right arm beneath Nesta's knees and gently raised her.

He held her cradled in his arms and for a short while gazed silently at the still face; then he turned and walked slowly, still dazedly to the door. And nobody tried to stop him. Nobody even moved.

He pushed through the doors, turned left to the passageway and followed it to the alley. His horse was there. He led it to a pile of whiskey kegs behind the Gold Standard, mounted them with her in his arms and got into the saddle. Carrying her as a mother would carry an injured child, he walked the horse down the alley and out on the open range.

CHAPTER TWELVE

THE SATURDAY STAGE

The whole of Redrock County was seething. News of the double shooting in the Gold Standard had spread with the speed of a prairie fire and citizens discussed it wherever two or more of them met. Eyewitnesses were surrounded as soon as they appeared on the street and the privacy of their homes was disturbed by questioning deputies.

The chief of these and the one to succeed Randall as sheriff was a short, stout man named Len Babcock. He was neither tough nor aggressive and prior to this had not been called upon to exercise any great amount of intelligence; now, thrust into a position of authority and with the death of the sheriff crying for the immediate apprehension of the Kid, he was seized with a sudden excess of zeal which carried with it a show of toughness and aggressiveness that was ninety percent bluff. The false front deceived nobody.

'What!' he bellowed when the witness who had taken the Kid's gun told of the affair. 'You mean to tell me you had the Kid disarmed and you not only let him walk out on you but gave him back his gun so's he could shoot somebody else?'

'That's just what I did, Len. Don't ask me why. The boy was so broke up that I just did it. If he'd needed a hoss to get away on I'd probably given him mine.'

Len glared at him angrily. 'I've a mind to run you in as an accessory.'

'Accessory my eye!' said the other scornfully. 'Go take a runnin' jump in a lake somewhere and cool off.'

There was no sorrow expressed or felt for Syd Randall. What sympathy there was went out, strangely enough, to the Kid. Randall had committed the unpardonable offense of shooting a woman. That Nesta was a dancehall girl made no difference; she was a woman in a land where women were scarce and therefore to be treasured and protected. And the sincere grief of the Kid had touched all who had witnessed it.

Jim heard the story when he returned to the homestead on Thursday night. Limpy told him while they unloaded the supplies he had fetched, and so absorbed did they become that they finally postponed the task until the tale finished.

Jim was grave. 'That's one shooting you can't blame Ed for. But it's too bad just the same. Syd makes his seventh, doesn't he?'

'If you feel like countin' him,' said Limpy shortly. 'Me, I don't figger him a whole man. Jest about a quarter, I'd say. The Kid done us a favor by rubbin' him out.'

'Who's acting sheriff?'

'Len Babcock. He's a sheep that's tryin' to play wolf and don't know the rules. He's chasin' all over the county after Ed. If he met him face to face he'd back up so fast he'd set his feet afire. I'll be diddely-dad-burned if I don't—'

'Ed sure is making it tougher for us all the time. He had to stumble into the Gold Standard and shoot Hal Turner right after I came back, and now—this.'

'Quit frettin'. They's one thing certain: when Kling hands Len Babcock that court order to put Dave off'n the Lazy L it won't be tore up. Len'll put him off if he has to call in the United States Cavalry. He's feelin' all proud and righteous and is gonna show the people of Redrock County how to run the sheriff's office, by grab!'

The probable truth of this prediction was

149

cheering. With the Lazy L in Jim's possession half the battle was won. He'd attend strictly to business, take care to offend no one, and let time work out his salvation. There were people in Redrock who had not entirely lost their sense of fair play; there were others who would be impressed by his evident desire to live in peace with his neighbors and who would eventually concede that one black sheep doesn't make a flock. And the threat to the Tepee would be removed.

Limpy had already started the construction of another shelter. He had felled trees, trimmed them and cut them to length, and had snaked the logs out of the hills with his lariat. It had been slow, hard work, but he had stuck to it doggedly, determined to make up for his weakness of Monday night. On Friday morning they went to work in earnest.

Nancy rode over that afternoon and Jim ceased his labors for a short chat with her. She had, of course, heard all about the affair in Springwater and her sympathy was all for Ed.

'Folks say that it was a punishment for the life he's led,' she said thoughtfully, 'and maybe they're right. But, Jimmie, think how he must have felt when—when Randall's bullet struck her. Poor girl! And they were so terribly in love. I can't help wondering what would have happened if he had gotten away with her. Maybe she would have changed him.'

'Maybe.' Jim was very sober. 'What I'm wondering is what her death is going to do to him. He'll either fold right up and lose interest in everything or go on the prod proper.'

'Folks seem to expect the latter. Naturally he's bitter, and when Ed's bitter he turns savage. They think his rage will be directed at Springwater and Ed Hall's organizing the men of the town. Dad's afraid he might hold up the bank, and we deposited all our cash at Springwater after Ed cleaned out the one at Redrock. The Springwater bank is so much larger and stronger. Now we're thinking of transferring our balance to the First Bank of Sage.'

'Ed promised me he wouldn't stage another holdup in this state.'

'That was before Nesta was shot. He isn't in any mood to remember a promise like that now.'

'I guess you're right. It might be a good idea to put at least some of your money in the Sage bank at that.'

'Don't forget that something over a thousand dollars of it is yours. I wouldn't want you to lose that, Jimmie; you're going to need it.'

'Half of it is yours, Nancy. I told you that before. You use your judgment about where to keep it.'

She smiled at him. 'Tomorrow's Saturday. The stage gets in at ten. Do you think the deed will be on it?'

'I'm almost sure it will be. Unless Pop didn't go to Hartsville to pick up his mail, or something happened to delay his answer.'

'I'll be on hand, then. If it comes I'll fetch it right over.'

She left and Jim went back to work. Now that the climax was approaching time seemed to drag. He worked the harder in order to keep mind and body completely absorbed. Funny that this sheet of paper should seem so important to him. But it did. It had become the paramount issue in this battle of his, and if it failed to arrive on the morrow's stage there would be another week of anxious waiting before him. Had he known that it was going to affect him this way he would have ridden to Hartsville and attended to the matter in person; but he hadn't known, and it seemed best to stay on the job.

He went back to work after supper, refusing to allow Limpy to help him, and kept going until dark. It was difficult to find relief in sleep, but he was tired and eventually succeeded. He was up at dawn and went to work at once, glancing often at the sun, mentally estimating how long it would be until the stage rumbled past on its way to Sage. If it was on time it should pass around ten-thirty.

But ten-thirty came and went and it had not rumbled by. Nor had it passed at eleven. Eleven-thirty came and went also and Jim concluded that the vehicle had had a breakdown. At last, just before twelve, it rounded the shoulder of hill and went rattling past, its six horses at a gallop in an effort to make up lost time.

Jim heaved a sigh of relief. Nancy would be along shortly. In half an hour at the most. And if there had been no hitch, she would have the deed to the Lazy L.

Tomorrow was Sunday; he would not go to Springwater until Monday. He supposed that Dave knew about his sending for the deed, for Kling would have told Randall and the sheriff would undoubtedly have passed the information along to Dave. Dave would naturally do everything in his power to prevent his getting the court order. He had probably instructed his father to scan every bit of mail that arrived in the office. There was a chance that Dave would guess that Jim would have his father send it to Tom Payne. There was also the chance that Jeb Culpepper might notice the return address of his father on the envelope. In either case would Jeb risk withholding the letter? Jim decided that he would. Jeb had invested his money in the ranch and would go to almost any length to protect his investment.

These two possibilities worried him. He had not seriously considered them when he wrote the letter. He wished now that he had written his father to mail the deed to Sage.

Limpy called him to come to dinner, and he ate hastily, one eye on the road. He finished the meal, rolled a cigarette and smoked it quickly. Limpy said, 'Loosen up, son. If the dad-ratted deed don't come this week it will next. Ain't as if—Here she comes!'

Jim glanced swiftly towards the road and saw Nancy. . .

*　　*　　*

Ten o'clock found Nancy pacing up and down the side-walk outside Jeb Culpepper's store. Some of Jim's anxiety had communicated itself to her; she knew how important the deed was to him and wanted to get her hands on it and take it to him.

Ten-thirty found her still pacing and no stage. She went into the store and started looking at various articles on display. She told herself that she was silly to let the thing affect her so; the stage had been late before and would probably be late again. The pull over the mountains was a tough one and hard on harness. At ten-forty-five she went out and walked some more. At five minutes of eleven she went back into the store and determinedly seated herself in a chair by the stove. At eleven the stage arrived.

She heard it rattle to a stop outside the store and saw Jeb Culpepper trot out dragging a mail pouch after him. She got up to follow him, then sat down again. He'd get the mail sack and fetch it in and then she must wait another fifteen minutes or so while he distributed the letters.

She heard voices outside and the pound of boots as men came running. She got up and hurried to the door. Redrock was just a stop to take on and discharge passengers and mail; the driver and guard did not leave their places during the short halt. But today both had climbed to the ground and were talking excitedly with Marshal Cliff Wood. There was a little group of men gathered about them, and off to one side were four passengers also surrounded by gaping citizens. She heard Cliff say, 'Come inside and tell me about it.' He came up the steps with the driver and guard at his heels. At the doorway he turned and said to a man behind him, 'Hold them outside the

155

store, Harry.'

Guard, driver and Cliff came into the store, and Jeb Culpepper trotted after them carrying three mail pouches. The one on top had a big slash in it. Cliff closed the door after him and turned to the driver. 'Now tell me about it, Hank.' They paid no attention to Nancy standing off at one side of the door.

Hank Stebbins, veteran of the reins, hitched his belt and plunged into the story.

'It happened on the other side of the hills, Cliff. You know how it is over there—up and down country, windin' road, timber. Wal, we coasted down a hill to what we call Turkey Holler. Road takes a wide bend to the nawth there and trees and brush are right thick. I swung the leaders into the bend and then seen a tree down across the trail. I set back on the reins and kicked on m'brake and we slid to a sorta sudden stop.

'It was right at the narrerest part of the road and no chance to drive around, so I cussed a bit and then told Milt here to crawl back atop the coach and git the axe we had lashed there. Figgered we'd lop off the bigger branches of the tree and then mebbe me and Milt and the three men passengers could swing her far enough to let us past.

'Milt laid his shotgun down on the seat and went back and started movin' luggage outa the

156

way when I suddenly seen that the tree hadn't fallen; it had been cut down. I yelled at Milt, and jest then a feller with a mask that covered his whole face stepped outa the woods and cut down on me with his Winchester. Me, I h'isted my hands right *pronto*.

'Wal, Milt started a scramble after his scatter-gun, but another masked feller stepped out on his side and cut down on Milt. A-a-and—'

'I h'isted my hands too,' said Milt. 'And kept 'em h'isted.'

'These fellers on foot?' asked Cliff.

'Yeah. But right off three more come outa the woods on hosses. All masked. One of 'em rid up and got Milt's gun and tossed it into the bushes then told Milt to chuck down the mailpouches and the specie box. We was carryin' five thousand over to the First Bank of Sage. Another of 'em herded the passengers over to one side of the road. Three men and a woman. Didn't bother the woman, but took the men's wallets.'

'Sounds like the Kid,' said Cliff.

'It was the Kid,' said Milt.

Hank went on with the story. 'The two that stepped out fust kept me and Milt covered. Two of the others started workin' on the strong box. They got it open and took out the money. Showed it to the one I reckon was the

157

Kid and he nodded towards his hoss and they put the money in his saddlebags.

'Meanwhile he'd slashed open the mail pouches and was examinin' the letters. He'd slit 'em open and look inside and if he seen money he'd put the letter to one side. When he'd finished, he gathered up the ones with money in 'em and put 'em in the saddlebags with the bank money.'

'Monkeyed with the mail, huh?' said Cliff. 'That's where he made his big mistake. Uncle Sam'll make him right sorry for that! Go on, Hank.'

'Ain't no more. One of 'em rode into the woods and come back leadin' the hosses of the two guards. The Kid waved the passengers back into the coach, and four of 'em lit off around the bend towards Springwater. The Kid—leastwise, Milt says it was the Kid—rode over to the coach and looked right hard at us through his mask and said, "If anybody moves for three minutes I'll send him where I sent Syd Randall!" Then he backed away and turned and rode around the bend, slowlike, not even lookin' back.'

'That's the Kid, damn him!' grated Cliff.

Milt finished it. 'I gathered up the mail and stuffed it into the pouches. Jeb'll hafta sort it all over again, I reckon. Hank and the men passengers hacked away at the tree until

158

they'd got it down to a size we could handle. We pushed it aside and got rollin' again.'

'And we gotta start rollin' some more,' said Hank. 'We're over an hour late and it's a long drag to Sage. Tell Jeb to hurry up with them mail sacks. Cliff, get word to whoever's actin' sheriff. Where is he?'

'Out somewhere lookin' for the Kid. He'll feel good when I tell him about this!'

They went outside and Nancy relaxed her taut muscles. She was thinking, *He only took the letters with money in them. He wouldn't take the deed.*

She waited some more.

Jeb came from behind the partition dragging mail pouches behind him. He went outside and called, 'Here they are, Milt!' The stage rolled on as he re-entered the store. 'Have the mail up in a minute,' he promised her.

Nancy resigned herself to wait some more. . .

Jim saw her ford the creek and ride toward him, and knew at once that something was wrong. She didn't hurry, and when she drew near he saw that her face was tight with disappointment. He clamped down tightly on his own emotions.

'It didn't come?' he said as she pulled up her pony.

She said, 'No.' And then she told him about the hold-up.

CHAPTER THIRTEEN

FLIGHT

Dave Culpepper and his crew of six rode into Redrock that evening. They left their horses at the store hitching rail and went their separate ways. Dave went into the store and drew his father away from a customer.

'That deed come?' he asked in a low voice.

'Nary a sign of it. No mail at all for Lawson and nothin' from Hartsville for Payne. Nothin' from Hartsville at all. You reckon he had it sent to Sage?'

'I don't think so. If he had, he'd have gone there to get it. He didn't. One of the boys scouted his place and saw him and Limpy puttin' up another shack.' He grinned. 'Not such a pretty one this time. Won't be as much fun burnin' it.'

'Maybe the Kid got the letter.'

'The Kid? Ed Lawson? How would he get it?'

'He held up the stage, robbed the passengers, took five thousand that was goin' to the bank at Sage and all the mail that had money in it.'

'No! Never knew the Kid to monkey with stages before. Better take your cash out of the bank. It ain't safe with the Kid on the prowl. What became of the mail that didn't have money in it?'

'They brought it here. I had to sort it all over. Come to think of it there wasn't anything in the Sage mail that looked like that deed.'

'Then it didn't come, unless Lawson's old man sent money with it. In that case the Kid kept it and he won't get a chance to give it to Lawson. That gives us another week. Lots of things can happen in a week.'

He went out whistling, almost colliding with Len Babcock.

Len said, 'Where's your boys?'

'Around town somewhere.'

'Get 'em together; I need a posse to go after the Kid.'

'This late in the day? It'd be dark before we got ten miles. And they've been ridin' all day lookin' for the Kid.'

'Where'd you look for him?'

'We combed the hills on the other side of the valley just on the chance that he'd holed up over there. And I mean we combed them.'

'What's the idea of combin' the hills down

161

here? I figger the Kid lit out for the state line.'

'Now that Nesta's dead I figgered he might hang around in Redrock Country aimin' to raise hell in Springwater and Redrock. We been lookin' for hidin' places, and I told the boys if they spotted him to shoot him like a sittin' duck.' He gave Len a significant look. 'It wouldn't be a bad idea to keep your eye sort of on that brother of his.'

'Jim? You got any reason for sayin' that?'

'Blood's thicker'n water. If the Kid gets in a jam Jim Lawson'll give him a lift and don't you forget it. He helped him escape once before and he'd do it again.'

He went down the street leaving Babcock thinking it over.

Jim and Limpy finished the hard work on the shack the following morning and Jim said, 'You might as well go back to the Tepee, Limpy. I won't need you next week and Tom probably does. You can make it in time for dinner.'

'Why don't you come along? Good chance to sample some of Nancy's cookin'.'

Jim declined. Sunday was Dave's day, and he knew that if he met Dave there'd probably be a fight. This was all right with him, but it might turn out to be embarrassing to the Paynes. Limpy rode off and he remained on the homestead putting the finishing touches to

162

the shack. He built a bunk and some cupboards and started laying up a stone chimney, using a bag of cement that had been left over.

He finished the chimney Monday afternoon and by that time was feeling a bit lonely, so he saddled up and rode to the Tepee. He arrived at the house an hour or so before suppertime but found nobody about the place. He sat on the gallery and smoked and in about ten minutes Nancy came riding into the yard.

She dropped from her pony and greeted him. 'I've been over to Springwater to draw out our money. Quite a few folks were making withdrawals. I guess Dad'll have to eat with the crew for the next two days; I want to take it to the bank at Sage and I'll have to stay overnight there ... Golly! I'd better get supper started. You'll stay, won't you, Jimmie?'

'Yes, thanks. Here; let me put up your pony for you.'

He took care of the horse, then went into the kitchen and chatted with her until the crew came in. He was convinced that the deed had not been on Saturday's stage because all letters without money in them had been delivered and he was sure there had been no cash in the one he expected.

Tom Payne came in and appeared to be

more cheerful than on the previous occasions. 'I think we're gettin' close to water, Jimmie,' he said. 'Some of the dust we pumped today was damp. I think that if we keep borin' in that same region we'll hit her.'

'I'm not doing anything this week; need any help?'

'Reckon not, thanks. It ain't a case of manpower; we just keep pokin' and hopin'. Nancy, you get the money?'

'Yes. I was telling Jimmie you'll have to eat with the crew tomorrow and the next day while I'm taking it to Sage.'

Tom sighed. 'I'll sure miss your cookin', honey.'

'Why not let me take it to Sage?' suggested Jim. 'I haven't a thing to do but wait for next Saturday to come.'

'Say, would you, Jimmie?'

'Sure I would. It would help to pass the time.'

Nancy said, 'One thousand twenty-four dollars and fifty cents is yours, Jimmie. Deposit it in your own name.'

He nodded, but he knew what he would do. Five hundred and twelve dollars and twenty-five cents would go to her credit.

When he left that night he took with him the money and a letter to the bank with Tom's signature attached. The amount was considerable, so he took up one of the large stones in his newly laid hearth, dug out the dirt until he had a good-sized hole, put the money into it and replaced the stone, taking pains to fill the cracks so that even a close examination would fail to suggest a hiding place beneath it. In the morning he ate breakfast, saddled his horse, lifted the stone and took out the sack of money, leaving the stone to be cemented into place when he returned.

As he forded the stream and climbed the bank to the road he had the impression that he was being watched. He scanned the opposite hill, but it was thickly wooded and would conceal a hundred watchers. His face tightened and he loosened the Winchester in its sheath. Responsibility rested heavily upon him; nothing must happen to the money that had been entrusted to him. He set out at the best pace his horse could make and turned in the saddle to look back at the top of every rise. The trail behind him was empty as far as he could see, but it twisted and turned and in places was fringed with trees and he knew that if anybody was following him he could conceal himself until Jim had passed over each crest.

He did not stop to eat or rest and reached Sage in time to get to the bank before it closed. He arranged for the deposits, took the checkbooks and passbooks and breathed a sigh of relief. Now if somebody felt like tangling with him let him hop to it.

He walked out of the bank and met Sheriff Trotter on the way in. They shook hands and the Sheriff asked him how he was making out.

Jim told him of the burning of his house and Trotter said, 'I wish I could do something about that, but you know what kind of co-operation I'd get from Sheriff Randall. Say! He's dead, isn't he? Heard about it. Can't say that I blame your brother for shooting him under the circumstances, but I'm sure honing to tangle with him just the same. The bank's pretty mad about that five thousand and some folks who were expecting money in the mail have been right disappointed. It's just a matter of time, Lawson. The Government's got men on the job now and they'll catch up with the Kid sooner or later. I'm sorry for your sake, but you'll be better off without him.'

Jim went to the hotel and engaged a room, then saw that his horse was stabled and cared for. He loafed around the town, had supper and a good night's rest, and started for home around eight o'clock in the morning.

He did not hurry, for there was no need for haste. He had pushed his horse hard the day before and now held him to a trail lope, slowing to a walk on the grades. At noon he was about two-thirds of the way home and pulled off the road to a grove of trees which sheltered a spring that he remembered from former trips. Here he staked out the horse, ate the cold lunch he had fetched, then sat with his back to a tree to enjoy a smoke.

The rapid drum of hoofs reached him and he listened for a moment with a frown of wonder on his forehead. Sounded like half a dozen riders going full out. As the sounds drew nearer he got to his feet and stood looking through the trees towards the road.

A band of horsemen swept into view and his jaws clamped tight at sight of them. There were six of them and they rode in a compact bunch, and the face of every man was hidden by a black mask. The masks had holes for the eyes and nose; the upper parts were tucked firmly beneath hats and the lower ends were held in place by knotted scarfs.

He muttered, 'Now what has Ed done!' and thought of the money he had deposited the day before. He said, 'Oh, God, not that!'

He didn't know what to do so he did nothing but smoke a cigarette and walk restlessly about. They had come from the direction of Sage. Something must have happened there, and they were taking this route through the mountains because it would be impossible for pursuers to cut around them and head them off. That much Jim was sure of. But what had they done?

The sounds of their flight died away and still he paced and smoked. He lingered now because he wanted as much distance as possible between him and them when he left. Damn Ed! He had promised to pull no more holdups in the state and he had broken his word. He had broken it when he had held up the stage; there was no doubt in Jim's mind that he had broken it again.

Whatever sympathy he had for his brother died then and there. It was Ed who had sent them from Redrock in disgrace; it was Ed who had indirectly killed their mother; now it was Ed who was ruining any chance Jim might have had to live down his thieving, bloody reputation. Brother or no brother, this was the end.

He picked up his saddle and strode to his horse. He would ride back towards Sage and meet the posse which was sure to follow and tell them what he had seen. Certainly they knew that Ed had taken this direction, but his story would assure them that the band had not turned off into the hills and would give them some estimate of the distance which separated them.

He did not have time to carry out his

resolve; he had just thrown the saddle over the horse when he heard again the rapid drum of hoofs. He hurried but they came too swiftly, and he turned and looked through the trees as they flashed by. There were ten of them, riding hard, with Sheriff Trotter leading them. Jim shouted but they did not hear.

He shrugged resignedly and finished cinching up. He gathered up the picket rope and coiled it and tied it to the horn. Then he mounted and rode slowly along the road. No need to hurry now.

The sounds of pursuit died away and the silence was broken only by the steady *clip, clop* of his horse's hoofs. He rode dejectedly, his eyes reflecting his misery. Suppose they had held up the bank!

It was midafternoon when at last he sighted the gap beyond which lay his homestead. Half an hour later he rounded the shoulder of hill and turned his horse towards the creek. He halted him abruptly, staring towards the shack. There were horses there, and men. he recognized Sheriff Trotter and Cliff Wood and Dave Culpepper.

He touched his horse with a spur and rode him across the ford and on to the shack. The men, he saw, were searching the place; they poked among the bushes and looked under the piles of scrap lumber and one of them was examining the rocks at the base of the cliff. As he approached they ceased their work and gathered in an ominous group around Trotter. Jim dismounted and said, 'What's wrong?'

'As though you don't know!' said Cliff Wood.

'I don't. You looking for something?'

There was no friendliness in Trotter's face now. 'Yes, we are. Where have you been? We didn't see you on the trail.'

'I'd pulled off the road to a spring to eat lunch and rest my horse. You passed while I was there.'

'Anybody else pass?'

'Yes. Six masked men. They were about half an hour ahead of you.'

Trotter was watching him through slitted eyes. 'Didn't you know the Sage bank was held up and cleaned out, did you?'

Jim sat down on the sawhorse, shoulders sagging. 'I guessed it.'

'You *guessed* it!' spat Cliff Wood. 'You *knew* it! Went into the bank yesterday and put some money in it so's you could size up the place and pass the word on to the Kid.'

Jim was too dispirited for resentment. 'No, I didn't. I deposited some money for myself and Tom Payne. I wouldn't have risked my own money if I knew the bank was going to be held up.'

'Why not? You knew you'd be gettin' it back today.'

That brought Jim to his feet. 'That's a damned lie! I tell you I had no idea there would be a holdup. I haven't seen Ed since—' He broke off abruptly and Cliff picked it right up.

'Yeah? Since when?'

'Since the night he held up the Gold Standard.'

This was not the truth. He had seen Ed on the mesa the following Thursday night, but he thought the lie justified. He said, 'What do you expect to find here?'

'Some of the money, if not all of it,' Trotter answered shortly. 'One of the gang rode over here. The prints of his horse are plain on the bank of the creek. The rest went on. His marks show that he rode after them later. What do you think he came here for?'

'To hide the loot,' said Cliff bluntly. 'Let's look some more.'

Trotter held out his hand. 'I'll take your gun, Lawson. Just in case. Stick with us for the time being.'

Jim slowly drew the Colt and handed it to him. Trotter felt him over for other weapons, then jerked his head towards the shack. 'Lead the way.'

Jim entered the cabin and they followed

171

him, crowding the little place.

Trotter said, 'I want every inch of this shack searched. Some of you tear that bunk apart. A couple of you get busy on those cupboards; there may be a hiding place behind them. Look for signs of fresh-dug earth on the floor.'

They got busy at once, swarming over the room like bees. The sheriff walked around the room, his eyes scanning the floor. He came to the fireplace and stood looking down at the hearth. Jim followed the direction of his gaze and felt a sudden stab of panic. The stone which he had left out of place had been put back and the cracks hurriedly chinked with earth. Would Trotter notice that it was dirt and not mortar?

Trotter did. He took out his knife, opened it and knelt by the hearth. He began digging the dirt from the cracks. He used the blade to pry the stone from its seat, grasped the edges with his fingers and turned it over on the hearth. He said, 'Ha!' and plunged his hand into the opening.

Jim did not wait to see what he had found. He knew what it would be. He was standing by the window. It was two feet square and there was no glass in it. He went through it head first.

He rolled once and came up on his feet,

running. Not towards his horse at the front, because they would expect him to do that, but towards the back where there was a space of possibly two feet between the solid rear wall and the rimrock.

He leaped into this space, jumped wildly over rocks and ran out on the other side. There were no windows in this side—just one in front and the one through which he had dived. He sprinted for the fissure on the far side of the park which led into the box canyon between the hills. His reason told him he was running into a trap but there was no other place to go, and he ran like a frightened deer seeking the first place that offered temporary sanctuary.

He heard yells from the direction of the shack, and presently the boom of hurried gunfire; but his instinctive action had completely fooled them. They had jammed the front doorway in their efforts to get out, and by the time Trotter had dropped the sack of gold and leaped to the window Jim had disappeared behind the shack. Once out of the house the men had raced around to the side by which he had escaped. They got tangled again in the narrow passage at the rear and one of them stumbled over a rock and clogged the passage. By the time they got clear and had sighted Jim he was on the far side of the park.

He felt a numbing blow on his shoulder that spun him halfway around before he could leap into the opening. He ran along the narrow ravine, nothing but bare, steep rock on either side. He ran for perhaps half a mile, leaping obstacles and keeping his footing only by the unconscious use of a brain and senses sharpened to acuteness by desperation. He came into the boxlike end, stopped, panting, and sent a swift searching glance along the rocky walls.

He saw it—a ledge ten feet from the ground and above that ledge another crevice in the rock. He did not stop to think or calculate; he just ran and leaped and his fingers grasped the edge and held like iron claws, and a spasmodic heave landed him sprawling on the ledge. He was up in a flash. The fissure was narrow; so narrow that had he considered before acting he might not have tried to make it. He turned sideways and squeezed into it and the breath was forced from his body by the tightness and he tore his coat and shirt and for one agonizing moment he could not budge. A last desperate heave took him through it.

A path angled upward, a path studded with ragged, jumbled rock; but he could see sky above and he scrambled to the top. There he paused to push rocks and boulders into the crack until he had blocked the opening so completely that nothing short of dynamite could blast a way; then he staggered across a rocky flat towards still more rocks.

And at last, miles away, panting with exertion, face stained with sweat and dirt, his shoulder a throbbing bleeding torture, he saw a cavelike opening in a pile of rocks and crawled into it like a dying animal and slumped down in utter exhaustion.

CHAPTER FOURTEEN

THE FUGITIVE

Dave Culpepper came riding into the Tepee yard shortly after supper that Tuesday evening. Nancy had finished the dishes and was sitting with her father on the gallery enjoying the cool twilight. Dave stepped from his saddle and Nancy said, 'Hello, Dave,' and her father grunted.

Dave put one foot on the gallery and observed her steadily. 'You heard the news?'

'What news?'

'About the bank holdup at Sage.'

'Oh, no!'

Tom Payne jerked upright in his chair. 'What's that?'

'Holdup at Sage. The Kid and five of his gang came dashin' into town like they always do. Three of 'em rushed into the bank while the other three kept people away. They cleaned out all the cash in sight and beat it, ridin' straight through town and onto the Redrock road.'

They stared at him, stunned, thinking of the money Jim had deposited for them and wondering whether the bank would have to close.

'How much did they get?' asked Tom.

'I don't know. Trotter said they made a right good job of it.' Elation crept into his voice. 'Jim Lawson was in on it.'

Nancy cried, 'Dave, that isn't so!'

'What do you mean, in on it?' asked Tom sharply.

'He spotted for the Kid. Went into the bank on Monday and deposited some money so's he could size the place up.'

'That isn't so! Jim rode to Sage to deposit some money for us.'

'Yeah? Then how come Trotter found nearly four thousand dollars of the bank's money under a stone in his fireplace? How come, after he'd rode up and Trotter had arrested him, he made a break and got away and right now is roamin' the hills without a hoss or gun or blankets or grub?'

'Keep talkin',' said Tom grimly. 'The whole thing.'

So Dave told them in detail. He said he and his Circle C crew had been combing the hills on the hunch that the Kid had holed up somewhere in Redrock County. They had finished a certain section and had returned to the ranch for dinner. He said he'd gone on to Redrock and was there when Trotter and his posse arrived.

'We figgered they cut around Redrock, for nobody saw or heard them; but Cliff Wood said they might have turned off on the road that runs behind the Circle C, so we rode back. Then Cliff pointed out Lawson's place and said that's where the Kid's brother lived. We rode over there and looked around. There were hoss tracks in the creek bank showin' where one of the bunch had cut over to the shack, and more tracks showin' where he had left. We went over and was lookin' around when Lawson rode up, cool as you please, and asked us what we were doin'. Trotter told him right quick.'

He went on to tell of Jim's apprehension and the search of the shack.

'Trotter raised a stone on the hearth and uncovered a hole with some of the loot in it. Jim musta known what he'd find, for he dived through a window and cut across the park to a little ravine that peters out back in the hills. Somewhow he managed to get out. They've been combin' them hills all afternoon but haven't found him yet.'

They sat in stunned silence and finally Tom said bitterly, 'And I thought he was a square-shooter! He ain't; he's just like his brother.'

'I don't believe it,' said Nancy firmly. 'There's something wrong somewhere. Jimmie couldn't have done it. I just know he couldn't.'

'You better get over that notion,' said Dave sharply. 'He saved the Kid when Tom had him cornered, didn't he? Blood's thicker'n water.'

'That was different. He might try to save Ed from hanging but he wouldn't steal or be a party to a robbery.'

'Tell that to Sheriff Trotter. Jim had him fooled, too. But he didn't stay fooled long.' He paused a moment to scan Nancy's face. 'What's wrong with you? You act like you was in love with the skunk.'

'Suppose I am?' she flared, and he jerked back as though she slapped him. For a short space he regarded her with smoldering eyes, then he said, 'In that case I reckon I'll be needin' that creek water right soon.'

Tom growled, 'She said supposin' she was in love with him; she didn't say she is. She's

178

all stirred up because we put our money in the bank.'

'Well,' said Dave tersely, 'she's been stallin' around long enough. I asked her to marry me half a dozen times and she keeps puttin' me off. I ain't one to be put off long. Nancy, you make up your mind one way or the other right quick. I'll be needin' that water in about a week.'

He turned abruptly, mounted his horse and went away at a fast lope.

Tom sighed. 'I reckon that finishes us, unless—You ain't in love with Jim, are you, honey?'

'Of course I am. I always have been. I didn't tell you about it because I thought it was plain enough. And I don't care what Dave says or what Sheriff Trotter thinks. Jimmie had no hand in that holdup. Why, Dad,' she exploded, 'you know Jimmie wouldn't offer to take our money to Sage if he knew the bank was going to be held up. He couldn't fall that low!'

'Like Dave said, it gave him an excuse to look the place over.'

'He didn't have to use *our* money. He could have gone in and got some gold changed if he wanted an excuse. Dad, I tell you he didn't do it.'

Tom sighed heavily. 'All right, honey.

Forget it.'

Nancy got up. 'I'm going to ride to Redrock. I've got to know what's happening.'

She went down to the corral. Limpy was hanging around and she asked him to catch up her pony. He stared at her. 'What's eatin' you, Nance? I'll be diddely-dad-burned if you don't look like a geranium that's been nipped by the frost.'

She said fiercely, 'I could kill that Dave Culpepper!'

'So could I, and a heap easier'n you. Jest say the word and I'll exterminate that dad-ratted son-of-a-polecat and consider it an honor and a privilege. What's he done now?'

She told the story of the holdup as Dave had related it. 'It isn't true! You know it isn't, Limpy! Jimmie's square; he'd never do a thing like that!'

Limpy was very sober. 'Shore he wouldn't, child. Now if they'd found the money on him—but they didn't. Somebody put it there.' Inspiration hit him. 'Say! Yuh reckon that dad-ratted brother of his'n knowed where he lived and figgered he needed some money and left it where he knowed Jim'd find it?'

Her eyes were wet, but she blinked away the tears and nodded her comprehension. 'And when Jim saw the sheriff take the money out of the hole he knew he could never explain—that nobody'd believe his story! So he got away while he had the chance and now he's wandering around in the hills, without a horse, without a gun, without food—' She broke off abruptly and lowered her face into her hands.

Limpy cleared his throat and said gruffly, 'Now you quit that. Ain't gonna do him a mite of good, your bawlin'. This yere thing needs talkin' over. Set down yere and put your back to the c'rral post and we'll hold a pow-wow.'

*   *   *

Jim could see through the cracks at the opening of his hideout that dusk was gathering. He had been lying in his cramped quarters for what seemed to have been many hours. At first he had been content simply to lie there and pant, but after a short while his breath had come more evenly, some of the feeling of exhaustion had gone and the sweat was dry on his face.

He had realized then that if he had noticed the opening in the rocks others might do so, especially since they would soon be combing the rock flat in search of him. He had crawled from his hiding place and had found a flat stone fifty or more pounds in weight and had managed to lug it in his good arm and prop it so that after he entered the tiny space it would fall against the opening and at least partly conceal it. Then he had waited with what resignation he could summon, knowing that he had done the best he could and that the outcome of the whole miserable affair lay in the laps of the gods.

The gods had been good to him; riders had crossed the flat many times, examining each jumble of rock as they passed, but they had not found him. The flinty ground yielded no telltale tracks and the flat rock leaning against the hole through which he had crept must have appeared to them natural enough. Several times riders had passed so close that he could hear their voices as they discussed his escape.

He had thrust his hand inside his shirt and had investigated the wound. A bullet had passed through his upper arm near the shoulder joint, and while he was sure no bone had been broken the wound had bled freely and pained with a dull incessant ache. His shirt and coat sleeves were wet and soggy and it was still bleeding. He tore a pocket handkerchief in two and stuffed the pieces between sleeve and wound openings. Then he stretched out on his back and tried to relax.

He wanted to smoke but did not dare to for fear the odor would betray his hiding place.

He did not underestimate his danger; if a posseman caught sight of him he was a gone goose. If they didn't shoot him outright the law would most certainly deal harshly with him. His relationship to Ed would count more heavily against him than would the evidence, which was damning enough. He did not regret making the break, although he knew it was tantamount to a confession of guilt. He wouldn't have stood a chance.

Damn Ed. Why had he chosen that place to hide his loot? It just couldn't have been coincidence. Jim remembered his sensation of being watched when he had started for Sage the day before. He had been watched. He believed now that Ed or one of his gang had been spying on him. But why the money? The only logical reason that he could find was that Ed, having in some way heard of his persecution, had got the idea that Jim needed money and had taken this means of supplying him.

Jim swore angrily. Did the damned fool think he'd accept the money knowing that it had been stolen?

And now at last darkness was falling and he must decide on his next move. For that move would have to be made during the night. He wasn't hungry but thirst tortured him. He had no horse, no gun, no blankets, no food. He had money but he might just as well have been on a desert island for all the good it would do him. He dared not go back to the cabin for, knowing his plight, they would most certainly have the place well guarded. If he tried to steal a horse from the corral on Dave Culpepper's Circle C and were caught, that would be the end of him. Nothing would please Dave more than to sock a slug into his heart and thus end forever the question of ranch ownership. He might try to make it to the Tepee, but the chances were that Dave at least would have thought of this possibility and provided against it. He was licked any way he moved, but still he had to move.

Then came the inspiration. The mesa! He knew every inch of it; there were hiding places known only to himself and Nancy. There was water there and edible roots and berries.

The twilight had turned to darkness but he waited another hour before starting out. He found his way to the crevice through which he had escaped from the box canyon and followed the lip of the ravine. The moon came up but the mountains bulked high on his right and he knew he could not be seen against the sky. He moved carefully so as not to dislodge any stones and send them clattering into the ravine below.

His progress was necessarily slow but

presently he found himself descending a
wooded slope and knew he was on the
shoulder of hill which formed one side of the
gap through which the road and the creek
passed. He had to cling to tree trunks and
bushes to prevent a too rapid descent. He
reached the bottom at last and saw the sheen
of the creek and the white ribbon which was
the moonlit road.

He got to hands and knees and crawled
down the bank and flattened himself against
the ground by the rushing water to watch and
listen. He saw and heard no sound to alarm
and finally crawled into the creek. When the
water closed over his back he swam, using his
feet and one good arm. He slithered up the
opposite bank and lay quietly at the edge of
the road. And then his blood turned to ice. A
horseman came into view, the animal walking,
the sound of its hoofs deadened by the dust of
the road. His figure was plain in the
moonlight.

Jim's first impulse was to slip back into the
creek, but he killed it at once. An object
moving in the water would surely be noticed;
even something motionless could be seen on
that bright surface. He was lying in grass and
a few straggling bushes; his only hope lay
right there. He bent his knees and gently
moved his muscles until his body was an

irregular black dot on the ground, then put his hands beneath him so that their whiteness would not show and buried his face in the grass. He wished for a hat to cover his head, but he had lost it in the wild flight along the ravine.

He could hear the slow *clip-clop* of hoofs now and the creak of leather and jingle of bit chains. He froze into utter immobility, waiting with wildly beating heart for the sudden halt that would tell of his discovery. It did not come. The hoofs seemed to pass right over him, then began to fade as the horse moved on down the road. As soon as he dared he turned his head and peeped over an arm. And then the horse halted.

He kept his head turned, watching. The man's back was to him and he remained motionless. Then came the flare of a match and the fear left Jim as he realized that the rider was lighting a cigarette. It came to him that now was the time to make his move; now, while the fellow would be blinded by the light. He got up in one swift, silent movement and walked rapidly but quietly across the road. He expelled a breath of relief when the shadows on the far side swallowed him.

He was at the edge of the road over which he had driven his cattle, the road which ran through the hills behind the Circle C. The moon did not penetrate here, and he walked swiftly, the sounds of his progress lost in the dust and sod.

He walked for an hour, the sky above him brightening as the moon rose higher. He found the path which ran to Lazy L range just south of the mesa and entered it. Another hour of climb and then descent brought him to the edge of the range and he waited there for some minutes scanning the valley floor for movement.

The mesa loomed ahead and to his left. It had at one time undoubtedly been part of the mountain range, but some upheaval had split it from its fellows and the erosion of centuries had widened the gap. The crack which split it from the bottom to the middle of the top was on the south side, his side. The trail which angled up the face of its western cliff would be directly in the moonlight. He had determined to ascend by the southern route. The going would be tough and it would be as dark as the inside of a black cat, but he knew that path as he knew the palm of his hand.

He moved out on the range at last, prepared to fall flat at sight of any moving object. About him were occasional mounds that he knew to be resting cattle; he circled them widely so as not to disturb them and finally plunged into the mouth of the great crevice. He reached the top after a laborious climb and moved directly towards the hiding place he sought. It was a cave in the side of a brush-choked ravine which he and Nancy had found and made habitable. The entrance was well concealed by brush and if he was careful not to disturb the branches and leaves he felt sure he would be safely hidden from even a careful searcher.

He found the mouth of the ravine and entered it, treading carefully. It was not as dark as he had expected it to be, for the moon was high, but he had to feel his way forward just the same.

A feeling of unease settled over him like a fog; his sharpened, alert senses told him that he was not alone on the mesa. There was nothing tangible, no sound or movement that he could detect, but the conviction could not be shaken off. He halted, peering through the blackness, listening.

A horse whinnied so close to him that he leaped back a yard. He stood rigid for the space of ten heartbeats peering into the black void, staining his ears. He distinguished a black blob that he knew must be the horse. He bent at the knees, his hand feeling about on the ground. He found a stone the size of his fist and picked it up. If they had trapped him there was only one thing to do—fight until he could no longer fight.

A voice spoke, low and distinct, and at its sound his knees turned to water. The voice said, 'Jimmie!' and the voice was Nancy's.

CHAPTER FOURTEEN

INSPIRATION

Jim loosened his fingers and dropped the stone. He said incredulously, 'Nancy! What are you doing here?'

'I thought of the pirate's cave. I knew—Oh, Jimmie, what's happened?'

He wheeled at the sound of footsteps behind him and Limpy's voice said, 'Jest me, feller. Ben kinda standin' guard. Figgered it was you climbin' the stairs on foot but I hadda be shore . . . Light up the parlor, Nance.'

Limpy joined him and they edged along the ravine and presently saw a faint aura of light on the foliage near the ground. Nancy had lighted a candle.

'Don't muss up the front curtains when you go in,' warned Limpy.

Jim got down on hands and knees and crawled through the opening to the cave. Once inside there was room to stand erect; he got up and gazed about him.

189

The cave was just as he remembered it, even to the stools he had made and the box which served as a table when he and Nancy shared their lunches.

He heard Limpy come through the opening behind him, then caught Nancy's exclamation of dismay. She was looking at him, an expression of concern on her face. 'Jimmie, you're hurt!'

'I'm more thirsty than hurt. I swam clear across the creek and forgot to open my mouth.' He laughed shakily.

She ran to a corner and he saw a filled sack and a canteen. She picked up the latter and hurried to him with it. He drank long and deep and thought he had never tasted anything so good.

She took the canteen from him and said, 'Sit down on the stool. I want to take a look at that wound. Shoulder, isn't it?'

He sat down and she gently drew the coat from his shoulders. She said, 'Limpy, your knife,' and when he had handed it to her she slit Jim's sleeve to the top, then along the shoulder seam. The wound was disclosed, swollen and red and encrusted with dried blood.

She said, 'Limpy, put some water in the bucket and heat it.'

He hurried out and Nancy said, 'I'll bet
190

you're starved. You can eat while I talk.' She went to the sack and started getting things out of it—a loaf of bread, butter, some meat, cans of various sorts.

'Dave came out to the ranch right after supper. He told us about the holdup and your capture and escape. I said I didn't believe you had a thing to do with the holdup and he didn't like it a bit. When he left I had a talk with Limpy and found he felt the same as I. We tried to figure out where you'd head for without a horse or supplies and I thought of the pirate's cave we used to play in. Remember, Jimmie?'

Her eyes were warm with the memory. Jim said, 'You bet I remember!'

'We decided that if we didn't find you tonight you'd eventually come here, so we got some things from the mess shack and fetched along an extra gun that Limpy had. If you hadn't been here we were going to leave the things in the cave and come over again tomorrow night.'

She had been spooning food onto a tin plate; now she set the plate on the box and moved it over in front of him. 'Hop to it, cowboy. We womenfolk like to see our men enjoy our grub. You'll have to skip the coffee tonight.'

He ate, savoring every bite. He said, 'Does

191

Tom know you came over here to look for me?'

'He thinks I went to Redrock. I told him I was going to ride over to find if there was any news of you. I intended going, too, but got talking with Limpy at the corral and changed my plan. Don't bother about Dad; the way Dave told the story he's inclined to believe you helped Ed in that holdup, but he'll change his mind when I get through with him.'

'Nancy,' he said miserably, 'your money—they took it.'

'What's a little money?' she said lightly.

'It wasn't a little money; it was a lot of money. But I didn't have any part in that holdup, Nancy. I swear I didn't.'

'You don't have to swear, Jimmie. I know you didn't. So does Limpy. Now eat. You can tell us about it when you've finished.'

By the time his appetite was satisfied Limpy was in the entrance pushing the bucket before him and swearing because he'd burned himself. Nancy set the empty plate aside and put the bucket of steaming water on the box. She said, 'We'll use the rest of your shirt for bandage; Limpy can fetch you another one.'

Her face was white but she went to work skillfully. She cleansed the wound thoroughly, Limpy helping her, and bandaged it with strips torn from his shirt.

Limpy went out to cleanse the bucket and cover the small fire he had built and Nancy asked, 'How does it feel?'

'Just like new. Nancy, I don't know what I would have done if you hadn't been here. I was pretty desperate. I wouldn't have gone to the Tepee because Dave might have been watching for me. The farthest I had figured was a good long drink of water and a meal of roots and berries.'

Limpy came back with a bucketful of fresh water from the spring and she said, 'Now tell us about it. Everything.'

So he related the whole story, beginning with the feeling he'd had of being watched when he first started for Sage. He told of the relief he'd felt when he'd finally deposited the money and his conviction that his imagination had been working overtime when he'd thought he was being watched. He told of his dismay when he saw the bunch of masked riders pass and his fear that they had robbed the bank. And finally he told of the finding of the money by Sheriff Trotter and his subsequent actions.

'I just had to get out of there, Nancy. Oh, I knew that running was the same as admitting that I was guilty, but if I hadn't run my name would have been mud. I can't imagine why Ed put that money there unless he thought I was broke and was trying to help me.'

'That's the way we figgered it,' said Limpy. 'The dad-ratted misguided ijit! Every way yuh jump yuh land in a tub of hot water b'iled by him.'

'Well, that's the story; but who will believe it?'

'I believe it,' said Nancy promptly. 'And so does Limpy. And Dad'll believe it when I tell him. But, Jimmie, what can we do? The only thing I can see is to get you clear out of the country.'

He shook his head. 'I'll stick it out here, Nancy. There's one ray of hope. Trotter said the Government had men after Ed because he tampered with the mail; if they catch him he can clear me. He'll do it; I know he will.'

'If they ketch him alive,' amended Limpy. 'It's a slim chance, but the only one short of provin' in some other way that yuh didn't help in that holdup.'

Nancy's lips were tight. 'We're going to try to do just that. I'm going to Sage and see Sheriff Trotter ... Limpy, we'd better be moving.' She got up from her stool and Limpy started for the opening. 'I think you have enough food to last several days, Jimmie. We'll be over and report just as soon as I get back from Sage. Keep your chin up, cowboy!'

He stood up and took her hand and looked

down at her. He didn't say anything, and she looked up at him and he saw in her eyes that faith that only a woman who loves can give. She smiled and pressed his hand and was gone. She rode to Sage the next day. She told her father of her meeting with Jim and of her faith in him. Her earnestness, together with the soundness of Jim's story, convinced Tom. He said. 'I don't blame you for helpin' the boy, honey; but watch your step. It'll be bad if you're caught at it.'

She rode slowly, viewing the terrain, trying to fix in her mind the sequence of events as related by Jimmie. Everything checked, even to the place where he had camped. He had described it to her and she found the tracks that his horse had made on entering and leaving. Her spirits were lighter when she entered Sage.

The bank was closed for the day, but there was no sign on the door saying that it had ceased operations. She breathed a sigh of thanks, asked where she could find the president, and called to see him. She told him frankly of Jim's involvement but did not disclose the fact that she knew where he was. To explain her interest she said, 'We're engaged to be married, Jimmie and I. I know he's innocent, Mr. Small, and I'm determined to clear him. I'm hoping you can help me. I wonder if you noticed him on Monday afternoon when he came in?' She described Jim's appearance as carefully as she could.

Mr. Small said, 'It happens that I did notice him. It was very close to three o'clock and I was sitting in my office with the door open and saw him come in. He entered in a hurry and went directly to the teller's window. He didn't even look around; just transacted his business and went out. If he was sizing up the place he was very cute about it.'

They talked a while longer, then Nancy thanked him and went out. At the hotel she questioned the clerk. He too remembered Jim. He had registered at three o'clock and stabled his horse. He'd sat in the lobby awhile and then went out. He came in again around five, went to his room and came down for supper at six. The clerk was relieved at that time and could not tell her what Jim had done after supper; but he had checked out at eight on Tuesday morning.

Nancy went out and questioned storekeepers. One of them remembered that Jimmie had come in and bought some tobacco around five-thirty. She wished she were a man so she could make a round of the saloons. Men found saloons good places to kill time.

She returned to the hotel and when she had had supper she talked to the night clerk. Yes,

196

he remembered Jim very well because he had remained in the lobby all evening, talking with various men and reading the paper. He had gone to bed around ten and had not come downstairs during the night.

Nancy got paper and pencil from him and went to her room. She wrote down all the statements she had received relative to Jim's movements from the time he had arrived at the bank until he left the hotel on Tuesday morning, attaching the names of the people who had given her the information. In the morning she went to the courthouse and saw Sheriff Trotter. She told him why she was interested in Jim and of her belief in his innocence.

Trotter said, 'If he was innocent, why did he run?'

She told him why. Because of his brother, Jim realized that he would be convicted without any doubt. She showed him her timetable of Jim's movements. 'Everything he did was open and aboveboard,' she said. 'Mr. Small told me the holdup was at ten o'clock; Jimmie was two-thirds of the way home then. On my way here I found the place where he camped. Mr. Trotter, I want you to ride out there with me and see for yourself.'

Trotter frowned. 'My dear young lady, that wouldn't do a bit of good.'

'But I want you to. It's dreadfully important. Please!'

He looked at her and saw the tears trembling on her lashes. He sighed and said, 'All right, if it'll make you feel any better.'

They rode rapidly, but it took them three hours to reach the place. They got off their horses and she showed him the tracks leading off the road. He looked at her sharply and said, 'Sure you didn't make these?'

She told him an indignant 'No!' He bent over and examined the marks carefully, then compared them with the prints made by her own pony. 'No,' he admitted, 'I reckon you didn't.'

They left their horses by the road and followed the bent and broken brush to the spring. The hole made by the picket pin was located, and they found the paper in which Jim's lunch had been wrapped. They also found the marks he had made while pacing about and the stubs of several cigarettes. They looked through the trees and could see a section of the road.

Trotter said, 'How do you know he camped here?'

'He left at eight and you did not pass him on the road. He must have camped at noon.'

'And what are you tryin' to prove?'

'That Jimmie had no part in the robbery.'

'Not in the actual holdup, no. We're not charging him with that. We think that he spotted for the Kid. Of course he didn't appear to be doing it, and your timetable accounts for a lot of the time he spent in Sage. But he could have met somebody when he left the hotel, or he could have passed his information to somebody he met on the trail after he left town. Maybe he did stop here to eat his lunch. Maybe he stopped here purposely to let them pass him.'

'But why should he ride to the shack when he saw you and your men there?'

'Because he couldn't see us until he'd come into sight himself. He knew that if he ran or kept goin' we'd be suspicious. He figured on us not finding that hiding place and ran a bluff.'

It was all so logical. Nancy's shoulders sagged and she leaned weakly against a tree trunk, blinking to keep back the tears of disappointment.

Trotter put a hand on her shoulder, cleared his throat and said, 'I'm sorry, Miss Payne. It sure is tough but you see how it is. I liked Jim Lawson; I sympathized with him when he told me he was fighting to make good. And then this happened and it looks very much like he'd made a monkey of me. And I don't particularly like to be made a monkey of.'

199

'He told you the truth!' she blazed. 'He worked and waited four years for the chance to come back and make good. And people wouldn't let him. They took his ranch, they ordered him out of Redrock and Springwater, they've done their best to make him line up with his brother Ed! And you're just like the rest of them.'

'Supposing you're right about him, how do you account for the money we found hidden under the stone on the hearth?'

'Ed must have put it there. Ed learned that they'd burned down his house and wanted to help him.'

The sheriff blinked. 'Say, you may be right about that. The Kid wouldn't figure like an honest man; he wouldn't be able to see anybody refusing money, no matter how it was come by.' He went on worriedly, 'I wish you hadn't come to me. You got me doubting now, and when I go after a man I want to be sure he's guilty.'

She brightened. 'Then you *will* help! You'll check up on his movements? Ask in the saloons; I couldn't go into them. Find out if he talked to any strangers.'

He shook his head. 'You sure are determined to clear him, aren't you? Yes, I'll check. For my own satisfaction.'

Nancy thanked him warmly and rode on to

the Tepee with a much lighter heart. She reached the ranch an hour or so before suppertime and sought out Limpy at once.

'Wal,' said Limpy when she had told him of her trip, 'what you've done shore helps. Gettin' the sheriff on our side means a lot. Now he'll be tryin' to prove Jim innocent instead of guilty. Not knowin'ly, he won't; but he'll do it just the same.' He gave her a sidelong glance. 'Dave was here, last evenin' and today. He seemed mighty interested in where yuh were. Tom told him you'd rid to Sage to see about the money Jim put in the bank.'

'I did see about it. The Kid fell down on the job; he just took the money in the teller's cage. We won't lose a cent.'

'Wal, that's one ray of sunlight in the dad-ratted sky. Reckon we're goin' over to see Jim tonight, and I figger we'd better wait until bedtime in case Dave comes snoopin' around.'

When Tom came in with the crew Nancy told him of her visit to Sage. Tom was not very optimistic.

'Even if you can prove where Jim went and when, it don't mean much, Honey. Wouldn't take but a minute to pass the word along.'

'I tell you Jimmie didn't do it!'

He chuckled and patted her shoulder. 'You say it just like that in the witness box, honey, and I'll bet a stack of blues the verdict'll be "Not guilty"!'

It was quite late when Nancy and Limpy set out for the mesa. They were very careful, Limpy scouting the ranch in all directions before they set out to be sure that nobody was watching them. They made their way into the wooded ravine and gave their prearranged signal. Jim lighted the candle and they crawled through the opening. He was transformed. He stood there smiling and with an eager light in his eyes.

He cried, 'Nancy, guess what! The black stallion's back!'

'Jimmie! He isn't!'

'Yep! I sneaked out for some water and saw him. He'd come up the west trail and had a bunch of mares with him. When he saw me he threw up his head and snorted just as though he was saying hello!'

'Jimmie, it's an omen! An omen of good luck!'

She told him of her visit to Sage, making the news sound as encouraging as she could. He nodded thoughtfully. 'We'll clear it up yet,' he said. Then, 'Nancy, I got an inspiration today. I was thinking about meeting up with Ed here on the mesa and I got to wondering what he was doing here. He said he'd come back to see Nesta again, but why should he hide out here when there are so many places nearer Springwater? I remembered something he'd told me. He said he had a nice little wad laid aside and some day was going to retire and enjoy it. Know what I think? I think he's got his loot buried here on the mesa! I think that's what brought him here that night—to bury the money he took from the Gold Standard. Nancy, I'm going to hunt for it. If I can find it and turn it over the authorities they might give me an even break!'

Her eyes were shining. 'Oh Jimmie, I believe you've got it! I really do! What do you think, Limpy?'

'I'll be diddely-dad-burned if I don't think you're right! I'll be a rip-roarin' son-of-a-wall-eyed billy goat if I don't!' He started for the entrance. 'You wait here, Nancy. I'm goin' back to the Tepee for a pick and a spade!'

CHAPTER SIXTEEN

LIMPY'S NIGHT TO HOWL

Jim began his search the next day. Armed with pick and shovel he started exploring the surface of the mesa. He did it methodically, beginning at the southwest corner and working north and south from the west to the east. He saw at once that the task was going to be a difficult one, for while Ed was fairly familiar with the mesa he had not taken the time to search out its many hiding places as had his younger brother and Nancy Payne.

Jim had scarcely started when he heard a wild flurry of hoofs and saw the black stallion and his band of mares racing towards the head of the trail which descended the split in the mesa. The black halted on a little rise, feet braced and nostrils distended, and blared his defiance, then tossed his mane and followed his band into the defile.

Jim grinned after him. 'You black devil! Want to play, don't you? Well, one of these days you're going to dodge down that trail and find the door at the bottom locked. And then we'll both have some fun.'

He soon found that carrying the pick and shovel was too much labor, so he returned to the cave and thereafter covered ground much more rapidly. Even then it was slow work; he had to investigate every bush, for one of the cleverest ways of hiding loot that he could think of was by taking up a whole shrub or tree and hiding it beneath the roots. When noon came he had not finished half of the area to be explored.

He ate a quick lunch and went back to work, and towards midafternoon came to a thin clump of saplings with a cleared space in their middle. His heart leaped when he saw a mound of freshly turned earth marked with two sticks lashed together in the form of a cross. He pushed through the underbrush and stopped abruptly. The treasure which lay buried beneath that mound was far more precious to Ed than any amount of gold. On the cross at its head was crudely carved the name NESTA.

He stood for a moment in awed silence. So this was where Ed had carried her when he left Springwater with her body cradled in his arms. He had remembered the one spot where her grave would remain sacred, the mesa near his boyhood home. Over twenty miles he had carried her through the night.

A spade leaned against a tree and Jim moved slowly to it and saw burned on its handle a Circle with a C within, Dave Culpepper's brand. The Kid had left her here to ride to the Circle C and steal the spade with which to dig her grave.

Jim moved silently away and resumed his search. He had not finished it when the sun dropped behind the hills on the west side of the valley. He went to the hollow where he and Ed had built their fire, cooked some supper and ate it. He was disappointed at his failure to find the money, but not discouraged. Ed was clever and the money would be securely hidden. Jim did not expect to find it without some trouble.

He knew that Nancy and Limpy would not be over tonight. Their luck had been good and they did not want to crowd it. Dave Culpepper was ever a menace; although they took every precaution it was natural to assume that Dave suspected them and would watch them carefully. Jim sat in the twilight and smoked, depending upon his ears to warn him of the approach of a searcher. This was Friday; tomorrow a mail stage from the east would drive into Redrock and Nancy would get the Tepee mail and scan it for a letter containing the deed. If it had not been mailed last week it would most certainly arrive tomorrow. His face tightened. Little good it would do him now.

He went back to work on Saturday morning and finished his examination of the mesa's surface. Outside of Nesta's grave there was no place that showed the mark of a spade. There remained hiding places to be ferreted out: piles of rocks with little pockets in them, the gullies which crisscrossed the mesa, the huge split itself with its jumble of rock and niches in its walls. Jim tackled the task determinedly, starting once more at the southwest corner. This was much slower work, and when noon came he had not covered a quarter of the upper surface.

He had just eaten his lunch when he heard a horse ascending the ravine trail. He went into the cave and remained there until he heard Nancy's signal. He went out to join her. Her face was tight and when he glanced questioningly at her she shook her head. The deed had not come.

'Ed must have taken it after all,' she said.

'I don't think so. If Ed was concerned enough to leave money for me he'd certainly know how important the deed is. He'd find some way of getting it to me. He'd put it in another envelope and mail it to your father. It's Jeb Culpepper who got it. He must have seen Pop's return address and guessed what was in the envelope.'

'But that's a Federal offense!'

'What would he care? He'd take the chance rather than let the ranch where he'd invested so much money fall into my hands. And who could trace the theft to him after Ed had already opened the mail?'

'You—haven't had any luck?'

'Not yet. I've been all over the mesa looking for signs but haven't found a thing but Nesta's grave.'

'Nesta's grave!'

He told her about it and led her to the place. 'There's just a chance that Ed buried the gold here, but I won't look except as a last resort.'

'I don't think he did, Jimmie. Nesta was something very precious; he wouldn't do a thing like that.'

'That's the way I figured it. I'm looking for hiding places now, among the rocks or in the sides of gullies. It's a big job but I'm sure the money is here somewhere. About the deed, don't feel too bad; it doesn't amount to a thing. If I ever clear myself I'll ride to Hartsville and get a duplicate from Pop; if I don't I won't be needing the ranch.'

She left almost at once, haunted by the fear that somebody might have seen her come to the mesa. He went back to work. All afternoon he searched and when the darkness came he had not found so much as a copper penny . . .

★   ★   ★

Shortly before noon, Tom Payne straightened, mopped his sweaty face and said to the crew about him, 'We're goin' to knock off for the day, boys. You've worked hard and steady for weeks and you're due a holiday. I'll pay off and you can ride to town and have

208

some fun. Tomorrow's Sunday, but if you feel like it we'll tackle her again. We're goin' deep this time, deeper than we've ever gone before. If we don't find her this time we might as well admit we're licked.'

They were drilling in a depression in the range, a hollow near the foot of the mountains which Tom had selected on the theory, right or wrong, that the lower they were when they started the closer they'd be to any water which might lie under the surface. There was nothing scientific about either their explorations or their drilling; they simply 'poked and hoped,' as Tom had put it. They were cattlemen, not engineers.

The crew greeted the news of a holiday with grins and muttered approval.

'We'll turn out in the mornin', Tom,' said Skip Sanborn. 'Water can't be more'n a mile away, even if it is straight down.'

They started to town immediately after dinner. Limpy went with them. He had been wanting to go to Redrock for two weeks, ever since that Saturday night when Cliff Wood had batted him around with a blackjack. Limpy hadn't forgotten that batting. He wanted to go to Redrock and find Cliff Wood and pay him back. With interest. Before he left he got a strong woolen sock and filled it with sand. Then he knotted it tightly, to keep the sand in and to give him a better grip. He put it into his hip pocket and felt good.

It seemed at first as though he might be cheated of his revenge. Cliff was not in town and Bud Falk told him the marshal had ridden off with Len Babcock in search of young Lawson. There was nothing to do but wait. He could wait there at the bar and probably drink himself insensible before Cliff returned, or he could wait somewhere else. He got into a poker game with four of the Tepee crew, but since one can't play poker intelligently without a drink at his elbow, twilight found Limpy pretty well loaded and primed for trouble.

Supper took off the edge and he had to start all over again. He did it at the bar this time and had a fairly good head of steam up when things started.

The Tepee boys were also at the bar and gradually the conversation drifted around to the Kid and his younger brother. Somebody made a slighting remark about Jim, and Skip Sanborn resented it. Words were exchanged and when their vocabularies were exhausted they continued the argument with fists. They flew at each other like Bengal tigers and the patrons immediately formed a three deep circle about them and started laying bets on the outcome.

Limpy was at the far end of the bar and was too late to get a good place. He wasn't very big anyhow, and he hopped about the outside of the crowd like a frog on a hot skillet peering between heads and over shoulders in an effort to see. He was rudely thrust aside by a big man who elbowed through the crowd shouting, 'Break it up, you two! Break it up, I say!'

The big man was Cliff Wood.

Cliff was swallowed by the crowd before Limpy could get the loaded sock from his pocket, let alone hit Cliff with it, but he was not to be cheated. He glanced about swiftly, saw the heavy lamp which hung from chains stapled to the ceiling and charted an aerial route to Cliff.

His brain, stimulated by alcohol, directed him in two short hops to the bar. He put his hands upon it and, with surprising agility, vaulted to its top. He took a couple of running steps and leaped, his fingers fastening on the lamp brackets. Under his momentum the lamp swung out over the crowd and when it reached the end of the arc Limpy kicked out like a kid picking up speed on a swing.

The lamp swung back over the bar so far that Limpy bumped his head on the ceiling, then once more swung forward. Limpy gave a wild yell and let her go. He sailed through the air, legs spread, and landed astraddle Cliff's shoulders. Instantly he thrust his feet under Cliff's arms and hooked his toes behind Cliff's back.

Cliff staggered forward under the suddenly applied weight, then snatched out his gun and thrust it upward in the general direction of the unknown horror which had landed on his back. Limpy promptly jerked the weapon from his hand and tossed it out over the crowd. They were staring, and even the two fighters were gazing at him, throwing their punches halfheartedly and without aiming.

The fight was forgotten by both spectators and contestants. Somebody yelled, 'Ride him, cowboy!'

Cliff was going through the antics of a clumsy bronc trying to unseat its rider. He whirled and he stumbled about, giving little up-and-down hops which were designed to jolt Limpy loose. But Limpy clung like a leech. Men began to shout encouragement and to laugh. One of them called, 'Two to one says he rides him out!'

The bet was taken instantly and more offers filled the air.

Limpy pulled the loaded sock from his pocket and started pounding Cliff on the head with it. The blows were interspersed with recriminations.

'Yuh will (*bop*) bust me with a blackjack, (*bop*) will yuh! Thought yuh'd make me talk, (*bop*) didn't yuh? (*bop*) Yuh dad-ratted son of a (*bop*) pie-eyed centipede! (*bop*) Take that and see how yuh like it!' (*bop*)

The last *bop* was too much for even Cliff's hard head. He stumbled to his knees and Limpy's weight carried him to the floor. Limpy sprawled out ahead of him but he broke the fall with his hands and kept his feet firmly twisted about Cliff. He pushed himself up until he was astraddle Cliff's neck and this time he brought the sock down hard. There was a final *bop* and Cliff went as limp as a dead fish.

Limpy disengaged his legs and staggered to his feet. His eyes were blazing and his chin was outthrust. He shrilled, 'He's my meat! Don't nobody try to take him from me!' Nobody wanted to. Limpy jumped between Cliff's spread legs, bent over and came up with a foot under each arm. 'Grab a shoulder, Skip! Git the other one, Baldy! By Judas, this is one diddely-dad-burned Sattiday night that Redrock's marshal is gonna be plumb outa circulation!'

Baldy, grinning, leaped forward and seized an arm; Skip, also grinning, grabbed the other. They lifted Cliff and started for the door. Limpy pushed through yelling,

213

'Gangway! Gangway for the percession! Mourners fetch up in the drag!'

They staggered along the street, a curious, grinning mob after them. It was less than a block to the jail; Limpy kicked the office door open and went in. He marched through the open corridor doorway and into the cell room. The four cells were empty, their doors standing wide. Limpy led the way into the first one on his left, said, 'Dump him!' and they lowered Cliff to the floor.

Limpy sprinted into the office and came back with the keys. He slammed the cell door and locked it, then went back to the office and searched the desk until he found the spare set of keys. Leading his triumphant companions, he wove his way back to the saloon. There was a watering trough there. He slipped up beside it and dropped the keys into the water. It was dark and nobody saw him do it.

They went whooping into the saloon and Limpy slammed a twenty-dollar gold piece on the bar. 'Drinks for everybody!' he yelled. 'I'm a dad-ratted curly wolf and it's my night to howl! Belly up and call your shots. *Whoope-e-e!*'

They were going strong when Tom Payne pushed through the doors. He called, 'All Tepee men outside! The back door and make it fast!'

Limpy turned and said, ''Lo, Tom. Have a drink. I jest tuk first prize at the rodeo. Rode a jackass to a standstill! Hey! Wha'ssa idea?'

For Tom had seized him by collar and breeches seat and was giving him the bum's rush towards the back door. Tom said in a fierce whisper, 'You old catamount, you've raised enough hell! Dave Culpepper and his gang just rode in and if they catch you they'll draw and quarter you.'

In the dark alley he spoke quickly to his men. 'We're gettin' out of town fast. Dave and his bunch just rode in and I don't want a fight. Filter out front and get your hosses when they go into the saloon. And Limpy, you'd better start layin' down tracks for Mexico!'

      ★   ★   ★

They went back to drilling the next morning. They worked desultorily and without enthusiasm. The excitement was over and they had hangovers. It was a hell of a world.

And then suddenly the clouds broke away and the sun came out and the birds began to sing. They pulled up the drill, section by section, to examine the point; and as they lifted the last piece from the bore there came a rumbling rushing roar and a jet of water spouted high into the air, was broken by the

215

wind, and came sprinkling down on them like a cloudburst. For a moment they stood stunned, gazing at each other foolishly, then Skip said, 'It's water!' The way he said it, it might have been whiskey.

Then they started shouting and dancing.

And just about that time Dave Culpepper came riding into the Tepee yard. Nancy heard him and came to the gallery, and she saw at once that Dave was mad. His face was tight and he was scowling. He dropped off his horse and came striding up to the gallery. He didn't say goodmorning or tip his hat. He glared up at Nancy and said, 'Where's Limpy?'

She was fed up with him. She said coldly, 'What do you want with him?'

'He jumped on Cliff Wood's back last night and hammered him unconscious. Then he locked him in a cell and threw away the keys. We had to saw him out.'

'I'm very glad to hear it. It's no more than Cliff had coming. Or have you forgotten what he did to poor old Limpy two weeks ago?'

'I mighta known you'd take up for the old coot. Just like you take up for that thievin' Jim Lawson. Can't tell me a man without a hoss or a gun or any grub can roam around all this time and not be caught. I'll bet everything I got that you know where he is and are keepin' him supplied.'

216

'If you rode over to quarrel with me, Dave, you might just as well ride back. I'll not talk to you while you're in your present mood.'

'No, I didn't come over to fight,' he snarled. 'I come over to tell you that I'm through babyin' you and your old man. I ain't waitin' until next week; I'm turnin' that creek tomorrow.'

He turned and strode back towards his horse, and Nancy watched him, appalled at the disaster which faced them. And then both heard a distant shout, a chorus of them, and both turned to look.

Coming at an all-out gallop were the Tepee crew. They were yelling and waving their hats, and suddenly a great jubilance filled her. Her father rode in front, and when they had approached near enough she saw that his big, kindly face was shining. The men were laughing and singing. Even Dave stared.

They pulled up their horses in a swirl of dust and Tom dropped from his saddle and came walking over to the gallery. His eyes went to Nancy, and then to Dave; and what he saw wiped the kindliness and good humor from his face.

He stopped and the crew were silent. He said, 'You two havin' trouble?'

Nancy said, 'Not at all, Dad. Dave just rode over to tell us he needed the water in the creek and is going to divert it tomorrow.'

Tom took two steps towards Dave and then checked himself. He said quietly, 'Get on that hoss and ride, Dave. And don't come back. Ever. Turn that creek inside out if you want to. We don't need it.' He turned to Nancy and the smile came back. 'We hit her, honey. We got a lake back there as big as the Atlantic Ocean and it's gettin' bigger by the minute.'

CHAPTER SEVENTEEN

HOPE AND DESPAIR

When Sunday noon arrived and Jim had not found the money, discouragement began gnawing at him. He had pried into what seemed to have been a million hiding places and he had another million or so to investigate and failure was getting him down. The thought which bothered him was that he had in some manner missed the hiding place, had overlooked some niche or crevice which contained the fruits of Ed's wickedness. He knew he could not drive himself to repeat the laborious search.

He stopped at last and gave himself a talking to. 'I'm not going at this right,' he told himself aloud. 'Ed used his head to figure out a place to hide that money; he didn't simply stumble on one. Maybe if I use my head instead of my eyes and fingers I'll get somewhere.'

He walked to the fringe of trees which surrounded the hollow where he did his cooking. 'Here,' he said, still speaking aloud, 'is where I met Ed that night. We went into the hollow and built a fire. Ed's horse was in the trees on the other side. The hiding place must be somewhere near.'

He studied the ground and peered behind bushes. But he had done that before. He'd even looked for a hollow tree and hadn't found one. He walked through the trees and to the bottom of the hollow and sat down on a stone near the black embers of the fire. He looked about him again, carefully, taking his time, letting his gaze dwell on each bush and tree and stone. There were none he hadn't thoroughly examined, and at last he gave it up. Might as well boil some coffee and fix something to eat. He wasn't hungry but it was dinnertime and habit is strong. He got some dry sticks and started stacking them over the dead embers.

And suddenly a hunch hit him so hard it jarred him, and he stopped all motion and knelt there staring. The perfect hiding place had just occurred to him and he realized that he had searched everywhere but there. He got up and ran to the cave and came out with the spade. He kicked aside sticks and dead embers and started to dig. The earth was hard on the surface where the fire had baked it, but when he had penetrated that crust he found the ground soft and loose. He dug feverishly, throwing the dirt to one side, and presently the spade struck something that wasn't earth. He dropped to his knees and started pawing like a dog unearthing a bone.

A patch of dirty white came into view and he gave an exclamation of triumph. He scooped harder. The white patch was cloth! He seized it and tugged and it came out of the hole. It was a flour sack and he knew even before he looked into it that it had money in it. He remembered that the Kid had put the money from the Gold Standard into a sack like this.

He set it to one side and continued to dig. There were other sacks in the hole; canvas, a couple of them; and also some buckskin pokes such as miners used for gold dust. He removed them one by one and put them on the ground beside him. At the bottom of the hole he found a bag that had rotted and fallen apart. There were moldy packages of bank notes and coins that had become tarnished.

The money from the Redrock bank holdup four years before?

Limpy had fetched him a hat to replace the one he had lost and he filled it with the loose money; then he took hat and bags and carried them to the cave and pushed them into it before him. He lighted the candle and went over his loot like a miser, counting it, keeping the amounts separate.

His hat contained a little over twenty thousand dollars and he was certain that it was the money stolen from the Redrock bank. There had been three men with the Kid on that occasion. One of them had been captured by Tom Payne as they were leaving town; the others had probably separated and the Kid had hidden all of the loot here on the mesa. He must have gone directly home from here, to be arrested by Sheriff Payne while eating dinner with the family. After his arrest the other two had drifted and had never come back for their share.

The money in one of the flour sacks, he felt sure, had been taken from the Gold Standard; the rest was the product of other raids made by the Kid. He did not know if the loot from the Sage bank was here, but there was nothing to indicate that any of it had been taken from the mail. Jim reasoned that Ed had had no chance to get to the mesa to hide it.

He emptied the gunny sack in which Nancy had brought the supplies and put the money into it. He was very happy. He went out and covered the hole in the earth and built a fire. His appetite had magically returned, and he cooked and ate a big dinner and whistled as he washed the dishes.

He expected a visit from Nancy that night. This was Sunday afternoon and Sunday afternoon was Dave's time. When, a couple of hours later, he heard horses ascending the trail he sought cover at once, never dreaming that the visitors could be Nancy and Limpy.

Her signal brought him from his hiding place, and when he stood up he saw that Nancy's face was shining and that Limpy wore a grin which stretched clear across his face. They dropped from their horses and Nancy came running to meet him.

'We've found water! Oceans of it! The boys struck an artesian well and it's made a regular lake!'

Limpy was hobbling back and forth, swinging his arms, too excited and happy to keep still. 'And she come in jest like a story in a fairy book,' he said. 'I'll be diddely-dad-burned if it didn't! Nancy'd jest got Dave told off good and proper and he was gonna turn the crick right then and there. And then Tom and the boys rid in with the news. And Tom told

Dave to git the hell off'n the Tepee and never come back. Son, I ain't never had so much fun since Grandma fell outa the hearse!'

Jim laughed with them and held out his arms, and Nancy ran to him and they hugged each other and danced about.

Limpy went on, 'And I had me a fine time last night, too. Reg'lar field day, it was! I hopped on Cliff Wood's neck and busted the daylight outa him with a sockful of sand, and when I'd hammered him down to my size I drug him to the jail and locked him in a cell and lost the keys. They hadda saw him out!'

Jim gave Nancy a final hug and held her away from him. His eyes were shining. 'You two aren't the only ones who had a good time. Nancy, I found the money!'

That called for some more hugs and a quick kiss or two. The kisses were given and received with little thought of their meaning. It was not until afterwards that either remembered them, and with remembrance came the startling realization that these were the first kisses they had ever exchanged.

They went into the cave and he showed them the money.

'All the cash taken from the Redrock bank and the Gold Standard is here. Nancy, this should go a long way towards killing the prejudice against me.'

'It will, Jimmie, it will! I'll take it straight to the County Attorney in Springwater. I'll make some kind of a deal with him. Surely they'll give you a break now!'

'I don't want you mixed up in it, Nancy. I want to turn it over myself and make my own deal. I've thought a lot about the best way to go about it. I won't give myself up now; if I do, it'll look like I'm trying to buy my freedom. I'll go to Springwater tonight. Len Babcock is a bachelor and lives alone; I'll give him the money and get his receipt for it and get out. Then when folks have been given back their money and are feeling in a better frame of mind, I'll surrender and stand trial for the Sage robbery.'

'I git it,' said Limpy. 'And you're plumb correct, son. Mebbe it won't git to folks right off, but sooner or later they'll be sayin', "Why'd he give up the *dinero* when he coulda kept it? If he's as bad as he's made out to be, why didn't he skip out with it and never say *boo*?" Yeah, I'll be diddely-dad-burned if yuh ain't right. Gittin' their money back'll make all the difference in the world. They'll be pullin' for yuh instead of ag'inst yuh.'

Nancy said, 'Yes, you're right, Jimmie. The case'll be tried at Sage, but that won't change the fact that you restored the money voluntarily. And the case against you is circumstantial; they found some of the loot in your house and you resisted arrest. But they'll listen to your story and they'll believe it. And I know Sheriff Trotter will help.'

'Yes, sir,' said Limpy, 'it's as sound as a hick'ry nut. Don't yuh go surrenderin' until we git a chance to start swingin' opinion yore way. Of course, they're some we won't swing—Dave Culpepper and Jeb, Cliff Wood, a few like Bud Falk and Hal Turner. But they're knowed as confirmed Lawson-haters and they won't count. Son, don't put it off another minute. Ride tonight. I'll fetch yuh a hoss soon's it's dark.'

They left shortly after that, doubly fearful now of being seen. Jim was still a fugitive and if he were caught with the loot in his possession he wouldn't have a chance in the trial to come. Even their testimony as to his good intentions would not save him for Limpy had aided him in many ways and Nancy had told in Sage that she and Jim were engaged to be married.

They were halfway to the Tepee when they saw a rider approaching them and recognized Dave Culpepper. They passed at some distance without speaking.

'Been over to see that water for hisself,' said Limpy. 'I don't like it, Nance, but maybe he'll figger we're jest takin' a ride.'

Dave did think that at first. Nancy was used to riding with him on Sunday afternoons and probably was following a habit of long standing. They had no doubt climbed to the top of the mesa. He rode on for a short distance, then reined in abruptly and stared at the huge bulk which rose before him. The mesa! Why hadn't he thought of it before? Finest hiding place in the world. Also the finest kind of a trap if Lawson were discovered there.

Dave rode into the ravine trail and followed it to the top.

Jim had heard him coming and had immediately gone into the cave. The searcher rode about for some time, once passing right by the cave. Jim did not hear him leave and did not venture out until dusk. A cautious scout convinced him that the person had gone, probably down the trail along the west side. It worried him a little but not too much. After he'd turned the money over to Len Babcock it wouldn't matter so much if he were caught.

An hour after dark he heard the sound of hoofs in the ravine path but kept to the cave until Limpy gave the regular signal. He went out quickly, taking the sack of money with him. He told Limpy of the searcher.

Limpy swore worriedly. 'Likely it was Dave Culpepper. We passed him on our way

226

home, the dad-ratted son-of-a-bowlegged-hyena!'

They made the descent together and reached the mouth of the trail without seeing or hearing anything suspicious. The moon had not come up yet and the range was dark. They waited inside the mouth of the ravine, straining eyes and ears but saw and heard nothing.

'Reckon the way's clear,' said Limpy. 'Good luck, feller.'

He struck out across the range in the hope of drawing away anyone who might be watching; Jim turned north towards the foot of the hills. When he reached the fringe of timber he followed it until he came to the trail which led to his homestead. When he reached the Redrock-Sage road he turned left. After a while he emerged from the hills to Lazy L range. Dave's ranch house lay to the south of him, but he could see no lights. He crossed the valley and circled Redrock in a wide detour which took time. When he was back on the Springwater road he halted to listen. From the direction of Redrock came the sound of hoofs.

Pursuers? He didn't know; but a body of horsemen traveling the road on a Sunday night was in itself suspicious. He put his horse to a gallop. At the end of half an hour he pulled up. The hoofbeats were nearer. Worried now, he sent the horse lunging on. The moon came up and shone on his back and when he turned in the saddle he could not see whether or not he was being followed. He stopped again in another thirty minutes, and now when he looked back he could see them, a compact group of shadows, coming swiftly. He could not be sure that they were chasing him, but he couldn't afford to take chances. He left the road and headed for some low timbered hills to his left. They followed, and now he was sure.

The money—he must get rid of it. Find a place to hide it. But he dared not stop and his horse was giving him every bit of speed it could. The trees drew nearer, a line of dark shadow ahead of him. Somewhere among them he must find a place. He heard a rifle bullet *zing* through the air above his head, but they were shooting from moving horses and a hit would be an accident. The horse came to a jolting stop at the edge of the trees, but Jim spurred him among them, putting him to a slow trot. They dodged around tree trunks, leaped over bushes and fallen branches. Jim peered about him in the dark, his eyes searching, probing. Behind him he heard the crash of underbrush beneath the feet of the pursuers' horses.

The trees were pine and scrub oak, and he had to duck low to avoid the branches. He turned right, trying to shake off pursuit. It was no go; they followed every movement doggedly, fanning out as they did so. He ducked a branch that suddenly appeared before him, then suddenly swung his horse against the trunk of the tree. He reached up and found a crotch. He thrust the sack into it and wedged it firmly in place. He glanced about swiftly, trying to get his bearings, to locate some landmark which would enable him to find the sack later. It was too dark to see anything that was distinctive; shapes merged into bulky shadows that in turn blended with each other. It was the best he could do.

He rode quickly on, his pursuers crowding him. He heard a voice shout, 'Better give up, Lawson! We got you!' It was Dave Culpepper's voice.

He cut right again, heading back towards the road. They swung with him. Some of them forced their horses to a run but he could not hear them because of the crack and rustle beneath his own horse's hoofs. He put the animal to a trot, still dodging and jumping. He saw the moonlit road ahead of him and gave his horse the spur. It leaped clear of the last trees and Jim saw three mounted men

229

waiting for him.

His hands flashed to the gun at his hip, came away again. Not that! He was the fugitive; if he shot a man it would be murder. He swung left into the road to make a run for it. He heard Dave yell, 'Take him alive!'

A noose settled about his shoulders and was jerked tight. He went off the running horse backwards and hit the ground with stunning force. Stars and sky and moonlight became suddenly a black void...

He opened his eyes and pain raked him from the back of his head to the soles of his feet. He tried to put his hands on the earth to push himself erect and found his wrists were linked together with handcuffs. He looked about him.

There were bulky shadows which he knew were horses and smaller shadows which were men. Some of the latter were hunkered down, smoking. There were six that he could see and at least two more behind him, for he could hear them talking. He identified them as Dave Culpepper and Cliff Wood. Dave said, 'Time he's wakin' up,' and Cliff said, 'I'll see.'

He heard footsteps and then Cliff was peering down at him. He gazed back steadily and Cliff said, 'He's awake.'

They pulled him to his feet and he groaned with pain.

Dave asked, 'He hurt bad?'

'Naw. Just shook up. Why in hell didn't you plug him?'

'And have people thinkin' I shot him to get his ranch? Not on your tintype. We'll let the law handle him. He won't be comin' back to bother us after ten years in the pen. Put him on his hoss.'

They lifted him into the saddle and tied his hands to the horn. They turned and started back towards Redrock He said, 'Where are you taking me?'

'Where they want you,' said Dave shortly. 'To Sage. Trotter'll be right glad to see you.'

They rode through Redrock, dark and quiet under the Sunday moon, and out into the valley. It was around midnight when they reached the ranch. They took him off his horse, caught up and rigged fresh mounts, then bound him to the saddle again. They rode at a trail lope, and it was eight in the morning when they entered Sage.

They rode to the courthouse with people staring after them, lifted him from the saddle and took him to Trotter's office. Dave said, 'Here he is, Trotter. Been hidin' on a mesa within a couple miles of my place. Been there all the time, I reckon. Nancy Payne and a jigger known as Limpy been keepin' him in grub. I seen them come down from there

231

yesterday and got a hunch. I posted my boys around the place and when he came down last night we followed him. He was makin' a getaway, all right. We caught up with him on the Redrock–Springwater road.'

Trotter said, 'Much obliged, Culpepper. There's a five-hundred-dollar reward; I'll see that you get it.' He raised his voice and called, 'Smitty!'

A lanky deputy came in from the next room. Trotter said, 'You boys are tired and hungry. I won't need you. If these are your handcuffs, Wood, you'd better take them along.'

Cliff slouched forward and unlocked the cuffs and put them into a hip pocket. The deputy started searching Jim. Trotter waved a hand. 'So long, boys; and thanks again.'

They went out and Jim heard their feet on the corridor floor. He heard them stamp down the outside steps. The deputy put the articles he had taken from Jim on the desk and Trotter said, 'Take him away.'

Jim stood looking at him for a moment, the story of what he had tried to do trembling on his lips. He closed his mouth firmly. No use. Trotter would not believe him. He went with the deputy through the doorway and along the hall to the cell room.

CHAPTER EIGHTEEN

THE SEARCH

The news spread. Dave and Cliff bore it to
Redrock and Cliff rode on to Springwater with
it. Miners in the gulches heard it, and
cowboys on the range. The Tepee punchers,
in Redrock to celebrate the finding of water,
carried it out to Nancy and Limpy and Tom.

They were appalled. The world had
disintegrated; the end had come. The capture
of Jim with the money in his possession could
culminate in only one way: a long term of
imprisonment which, to Jim, would be worse
than death.

But had they found the money? Rumor said
nothing about it, yet it was entirely clear that
Jim had been taken before he reached
Springwater. Had he managed to get rid of it?
If so, where? Nancy had to know. She and
Limpy saddled up and started at once for
Sage.

They reached Sage in the middle of the
afternoon and went immediately to Sheriff
Trotter's office. Trotter was sympathetic but
grim. Yes, they could see Jimmie; yes, they
could get him a lawyer. He'd certainly need

one. The circuit judge lived in Sage and would convene a special session of court to try the case. They hired a lawyer named James B. Kelly and returned to the sheriff's office with him. They were shown into the adjoining office and a guard brought in Jim. The guard went out and closed the door.

Nancy said, 'Jimmie, this is Mr. Kelly, the lawyer who's going to defend you. Jimmie, what happened? Sit down and tell us about it.'

Jim sat down and told them. He spoke slowly, in a voice that was dead. There was no hope in him. He was licked.

'And the money, Jimmie—what became of it?'

He gazed at her soberly. 'I hid it. In the first place I could find. But it doesn't matter now.'

'But it does! It does matter! If we get it and turn it over and tell what you had planned to do it will help!'

He smiled cynically. 'Who would believe you? It would look as though you were trying to buy me off; worse, it would show you and Limpy to be—' he said it bitterly—'my partners in crime.'

Kelly said, 'What's this about money?'

So Nancy told him and he began to sit up and take notice. Their story gave the case an entirely new aspect. He said at once, 'Of course we must get that money. Handled right it can win your freedom for you. Where did you hide it, Jim?'

'I don't know exactly. I turned off the road five, six miles the other side of Redrock. There were some low hills covered with pine and scrub oak on my left. I rode in among them a little distance, a hundred feet or so, and pushed it up among the branches of a tree. It was too dark to see any landmarks.'

'We must search for it right away. Did you tell Trotter about it?'

'I've told nobody. Let the word get out and every man in the country will be hunting for it. And not all of them would be honest.'

'Miss Payne, will you undertake the search?'

'Yes! Limpy and I. We want to, don't we, Limpy?'

'You're danged tootin'! And we'll find it, too.'

There were so anxious to get at it that they left immediately for home. They arrived at the Tepee after midnight and were up at dawn the next morning. Nancy had told her father, and Tom rode with them. The tension in Redrock had not lessened; they sensed it as they rode through the town. Jeb Culpepper was voicing his opinion to a group of men hanging about the store. Dave was there and gave them a leer as they passed.

'Everybody's sayin' I told yuh so, the dad-ratted fools,' growled Limpy. 'Jest wait till we find that money; them that's condemnin' the loudest 'll be fallin' all over Jim's neck when they git their *dinero* back.'

They looked for the hills Jim had described and to their dismay found that a line of them extended for miles beyond Redrock. They estimated where Jim had turned off the road and began their search. They found plenty of pines and scrub oaks but none of them with a flour sack hidden among its branches. They went about the work methodically and at the end of the day rode back to the Tepee steeped in discouragement. When they went out the next day they took camping equipment along with them.

They searched for a place where the underbrush had been trodden down, but cattle ranged over the whole area and there were many such places. They had started the search on Tuesday morning and they continued it through Thursday. On Thursday evening while they were eating a dismal supper, a Tepee cowboy rode up with the news that Jim's trial would start on the morrow.

They were dismayed. They had investigated every tree along the base of the hills from a mile outside of Redrock to a mile beyond the farthest point where Jim could have left the road. They hadn't found the money.

'Dad,' said Nancy in desperation, 'what'll we do? We've got to be at that trial, and yet—'

'You two go,' said Limpy. 'I'll stick on the job. I got me a idee. We've covered plenty territory east and west but we ain't gone no deeper than a couple hundred feet. Mebbe Jimmie miscalculated his distance. Remember he was excited and worried and tryin' to find a place to hide that there sack. And it was mighty dark among them trees. Mebbe he went in deeper'n he thought. I'm gonna start workin' nawth 'stead of east and west.'

Nancy and Tom and the whole Tepee crew rode to Sage the next day. They left at three in the morning in order to be on hand when court opened, but they found the traffic heavy. When they entered the courtroom it was filled with people from Redrock and Springwater. Dave Culpepper and his Circle C crew were there. A deputy stood at the entrance collecting guns and handing out checks.

Lawyer Kelly hurried to them, his eyebrows lifted inquiringly, anxiously.

Nancy shook her head. 'We didn't find it. Limpy's stll searching.'

Kelly said worriedly, 'We're sunk without

it. And there isn't much time. They're going to rush this case through. The prosecution plans to finish up this afternoon. I can kill some time when the jury is selected, but I can't stall too much without hurting our case. My only hope is to put Jim on the stand and let him tell his story. But I'm afraid he won't put his heart into it.'

A deputy brought Jim into the room, the judge entered and court was declared in session. The jury was selected and a recess was declared until one o'clock. They wouldn't let Nancy talk to Jim.

As soon as court reconvened, the prosecuting attorney went to work. He made a short speech outlining the case against Jim, then called to the stand Sheriff Trotter, Dave Culpepper and Cliff Wood. In spite of Kelly's objections the name of the Kid was mentioned time and time again. It didn't matter much; everybody knew that the Kid was Jim Lawson's brother. When the prosecution announced that it would rest, Nancy's face was white and anxious and Tom was grim. He had been through many a trial; he saw which way the balance swung.

It was three o'clock, Lawyer Kelly got to his feet and spoke gravely.

'I'm not going to waste the time of the court by calling witnesses to testify to the character of the defendant as they know it. I'm going to put James Lawson on the stand and let him tell his own story in his own words, trusting that his directness and sincerity will appeal to you as it did to me. And when he's finished, I want every one of you to remember that the case as built up by the prosecution is entirely circumstantial. Gold was found under a hearthstone in James Lawson's home. It was the gold stolen from the First Bank of Sage. I believe it was put there by the Kid, without Jim's knowledge, because the Kid knew Jim was being persecuted and believed that his brother needed it. It is true that Jim fled when the sheriff found that gold, but he did so because—'

The judge interrupted him. 'You can save that for your summing up, Counselor.'

Kelly bowed his submission. He said, 'James Lawson, take the stand.'

Jim sat down in the witness chair and was sworn. He was listless, almost uninterested. His attitude said there is no hope, why draw the thing out? He started talking in a dead voice, without expression, in a tone so low that his words could not be heard halfway across the courtroom. A girl's voice reached him, high-pitched, insistent.

'Jimmie! *Fight!*'

He jerked his head up, stung out of his

lethargy. Nancy! That was Nancy standing tense and white, her eyes pleading with him. Nancy, his playmate, his girl! And she'd said to fight!

The judge rapped smartly with his gavel. 'Be seated, Miss Payne. I'll have no interruptions.'

She sat down, slowly, her eyes still pleading. Jim straightened in his chair. His eyes brightened, grew hard; his jaws clamped together. He gripped the arms of the chair with tense fingers. All right, he'd fight!

He started over, but in a new voice; a voice that rang with sincerity. They could all hear him now. He told his story as he had lived it, making them feel every hurt that had been inflicted on him as a boy because of Ed, every bitter word that had cut. He told of their flight after the Kid's escape, of their long struggle to start anew, of his mother's death and his determination to return and live down the reputation of his brother. He told of his reception, of his finding the Lazy L in the hands of Dave Culpepper and of Dave's refusal to relinquish it.

People were sitting erect in their seats; the members of the jury were leaning forward in the box, intent upon every word. He told of the events leading up to his detention by Sheriff Trotter and of his flight. He told them of the two who waited for him on the mesa because they believed in him and loved him. And then he told of finding the hidden loot and for a few minutes after that the court was in an uproar.

Kelly, seizing the opportunity, leaped to his feet. When silence had been restored he said, 'What had you intended doing with that money? What, in fact, did you actually attempt to do?'

He told them. He was holding nothing back now. He told them of the pursuit and of his hiding the money so that he could get it later and finish his job of restoraton.

'Did you even tell Miss Payne and Limpy where to look for that money?'

'Yes. As nearly as I could. It was in the branches of a tree, but it was dark and I couldn't tell them the exact spot.'

Dave Culpepper shouted, 'That's a lie! He's sayin' that to get sympathy!'

A voice from the back of the courtroom answered him.

''Tain't no lie, neither! *Because I got that dad-ratted money right yere!*'

Limpy came hobbling down the aisle, a gunny sack hugged to his chest.

CHAPTER NINETEEN

WITNESS FOR
THE DEFENSE

Dave Culpepper stamped angrily into a saloon
near the courthouse, his six men at his heels.
The uproar following Limpy's arrival was
such that the judge had adjourned court until
ten o'clock the following day. Dave ordered
drinks for his crowd and said to the world in
general, 'The damned fools! You'd think he
was some kind of hero. Can't they see that he
was makin' a getaway with that cash? That his
havin' it makes him twice as guilty? Are they
all crazy?'

The man beside him said, 'Right now I
reckon they are. Tomorrow it'll be different.
The prosecutin' attorney'll see to that.'

Dave set his jaws tightly. 'Mebbe. But the
damage has been done. If the jury took a vote
right now he'd be acquitted twelve to nothin'.

'Trouble is,' he went on gloomily, 'they
ain't never had the Kid strike at 'em hard
enough over here. Nothin' but that puny little
bank robbery. If the Kid had killed somebody
they all know and liked they'd act different.
They wouldn't feel so kind towards Lawsons.'

'Suppose he does get acquitted?' asked one of them.

'If he does,' said Dave viciously, 'we'll all be lookin' for new jobs.'

He left them and went out on the street. The town was seething. Men gathered in groups and talked excitedly; sentiment had veered in Jim's favor. Lawyer Kelly, with Nancy at his side, passed Dave. They were laughing and talking happily. Tom and Limpy followed, faces shining. Dave growled an oath and turned away. Why hadn't the Kid killed somebody in Sage instead of Art Fenton?

He saw the prosecuting attorney come down the courthouse steps looking worried and went over to meet him. He said, 'I hope you ain't lettin' that fairy story about returnin' the money fool you. He wasn't goin' to turn that money in; he was clearin' out with it. Mebbe he did tell Nancy Payne and Limpy that he was, but he needed their help for the getaway. I tell you he was headed for the state line.'

'I thought of that,' said the prosecuting attorney. 'I'll bear down hard on it tomorrow. But right now it looks like an acquittal to me.'

Ten o'clock the next morning saw the courthouse jammed with spectators anxious to be in at the finish. The excitement of the previous day had faded and doubt had begun to creep in. They had had time to think over that part of the story dealing with the recovered money. After all, it had not been delivered to the authoritics; it had not been found until Jim's case looked utterly hopeless. The dramatic finish of Lawson's testimony might have been deliberately staged to win their sympathy. Dave and his men had been very busy the night before spreading their doctrine of hate.

The prosecuting attorney advanced to the witness chair to cross-examine Jim. His eyes were hard and his jaws were set belligerently. He said, 'Lawson, you said yesterday that you started for Springwater with the intention of turning that money over to the authorities. You knew your pursuers were on the side of the law; why didn't you turn the money over to them and give yourself up?'

'Dave Culpepper had stolen my ranch; I wouldn't put it past him to steal some thirty thousand dollars in cash.'

'You wouldn't, ch? Let's look at it from another angle. You had thirty thousand odd dollars in cash, a good horse under you, a gun, and Mexico and safety not far away. Are you sure, Lawson, that the remarkable urge to return that money didn't come to you *after* you knew you were going to be caught? Why did you pick night-time to return it? Why didn't you go to Redrock?' He leaned forward and spat the words at Jim. 'Why do you lie about that money? Isn't it true that you were making a getaway with it after telling Miss Payne and Limpy your sob story in order to get the horse and the gun? Didn't you hide that money in the hope of coming back for it later and keeping it for yourself?'

'No!' cried Jim. 'That isn't true! It's you who're lying when you say that!'

The prosecuting attorney straightened and expelled his breath.

'Very well. We'll leave the subject of the money and your noble impulse to return it for the jury to think about. We'll come back to the specific crime with which you are charged. Did you or did you not visit the First Bank of Sage on Monday, the day before it was held up?'

'Yes, I did. I—'

'And while you were in the bank isn't it true that you looked about you and noticed how the place was laid out, how many employees there were and where they were working, where the vault was located and whether it was open or closed?'

'No, I did not.'

'You didn't? I say you did! I say that you sized up the interior of the bank and later met

245

your brother or one of his infamous band and passed along the information to him. I say that your brother, known as the Kid, left his fleeing companions at the risk of being caught himself in order to put your share of the loot in a place where you could find it!'

'And that,' said a cold voice from the front of the courtroom, 'is another damned lie!'

The voice came from behind Jim, from behind and to one side of the judge's bench. It came from a doorway to the judge's chambers, a small room with a private entrance which opened on a passageway beside the building.

A man stood in the entrance to that little room. He held a Colt .45 in each hand and they were pointed at the deputy who guarded Jim and at Sheriff Trotter who sat just outside the railing. The man wore no mask, and everybody present knew him instantly. He was Edward Lawson, the Kid. He came gliding forward, walking on the balls of his feet like a tawny cougar, his gaze flicking out over the silent, staring room, his eyes restless.

'Don't nobody move or I'll turn this trial into a funeral.' He looked down at the astonished and frightened attorney. 'Mister, I said you lied. I put no money where Jim could find it. I don't even know where he hangs out.'

Lawyer Kelly sprang to his feet. 'My
246

witness, Your Honor! I'm calling Edward Lawson to the stand. Take the witness stand and be sworn, Mr. Lawson.'

Jim started to get out of the chair, but Ed motioned him back into it with one of his guns. 'Stay put, Jim. I'll do my talkin' from where I am and I'll talk without bein' sworn. And what I say will be the truth. On the day the Sage bank was held up I was nowhere near Sage. I was five hundred miles away, in another state.'

'You say it wasn't you and your gang who held up the Sage bank?' gasped Kelly.

'I had no gang then. I have no gang now. We busted up after—after Nesta—' A spasm of agony crossed his face. He blurted savagely, 'We busted up after I'd sent Syd Randall to hell where he belongs!'

'And the mail stage—you didn't hold that up?'

The Kid sneered. 'A letter from Aunt Minnie to her niece with a buck in it for her birthday! A sawbuck from some father to his son so's he could come home! Peanuts. I never stopped any mail stage. I wasn't even in the state when it was held up.'

'Then how do you explain the money that was found under a hearthstone in Jim Lawson's home?'

'A frame-up! Some dirty sidewinder

planted it there so that a bunch of crazy, prejudiced fools would find it and connect Jim with the robbery! Somebody that wanted to get rid of him; somebody that had tried other ways to get rid of him but failed because he had the guts to stick it out!'

'But who—?'

The sound of a shot interrupted him. It came from some distance down the street, muffled but unmistakable for what it was. There came two more in quick succession, and then another single one. Judge and attorneys, sheriff and deputies, witnesses and spectators sat rigid, listening. And then there came the sudden flurry of hoofs like a rolling drum in the distance. The sound grew rapidly louder and the floor trembled as a band of horsemen raced past the courthouse.

Trotter sprang to his feet and the Kid flipped up his gun and said, 'Sit down!' Trotter sat down slowly, reluctantly. The sound of hoofbeats diminished and died in the distance and nobody moved. Then came the slap of feet on the corridor floor and the door was flung open and a man came bursting into the room. He wore no hat and he was sweating with excitement and his eyes were like full moons.

He cried, 'Where's the sheriff? Where's Trotter? The Kid and his gang just held up the bank! And the Kid shot and killed Mr. Small as he was sittin' at his desk with his hands up!'

They stirred then, these who had been spellbound. They stirred with anger and sudden understanding. This man said the Kid had done it, and they knew that he hadn't. Because the Kid was standing on the platform looking down at them and he had been standing there when the shots were fired.

Jim was still in the witness chair and he could look out over the courtroom and the restless, surging crowd it held; but now he got to his feet in order to see the better. He was looking for a certain man and he could not find him and understanding reached him with the violence of a blow.

Again Trotter started to his feet and again the Kid cried, 'Sit down!'

Trotter protested angrily. 'You heard what that man said! The bank has been held up and Mr. Small shot at his desk! If you have any sense of justice left in that wicked heart of yours you'll let me go after them!'

'I reckon that to be my job. Mine and Jim's.' He said to his brother in a distinct voice, 'Come along, Jim. Out the side door. I got a hoss waitin' for you. Rustle your hocks!'

Jim didn't stop to figure out the right or wrong of it. He leaped out of the chair and

circled the Kid, and as he passed the Kid
thrust one of his guns into Jim's hand. Inside
the little room Jim paused until the Kid came
backing in. They leaped across the room and
through the doorway. Ed had a key in his
hand; he pulled the door shut and locked it.

They ran around the corner into the alley
and Jim saw two horses waiting there. They
jerked loose the reins and vaulted into the
saddles.

Ed said shortly, 'Dave Culpepper?'

Jim said, 'Yes. He and his men weren't in
the courtroom. Ed, this is the showdown!'

CHAPTER TWENTY

THE KID'S LAST RIDE

They rode hard, their one desire to come to
grips with Dave Culpepper. That Dave
probably had with him six hard men did not
dismay them; a savage hatred filled their
minds and crowded out all thoughts of odds.
Dave Culpepper, knowing the blame would
fall on the Kid, had held up the stage in order
to get the deed from the mail. Dave
Culpepper, seeing the balance of public
opinion swinging towards Jim, had committed

this final outrage in order to tip the scales the other way. Not until their horses were heaving and laboring did they diminish their pace. During the brief slowdown the brothers had their first chance to converse.

Ed said, 'We should have got near enough to see them by now if they'd kept the same hosses. Looks like they didn't.'

'How would they change?'

'Dave didn't think this up on the spur of the moment. Likely planned it last night and sent one of his men back to fetch fresh hosses to a halfway point on the trail. They switched and hazed the tired ones into one of them little parks and turned 'em loose.'

They spoke no more, chafing at the delay. When the horses had recovered some measure of strength they put them to a gallop once more. They rode past Jim's homestead and through the gap and finally emerged on Lazy L range. They looked towards the south and saw the buildings of Dave's ranch. There were no horses in the corral, no sign of anybody about the place. The road had been traveled so much in the last few days that there was nothing to be gained by studying it for tracks.

The Kid said, 'They coulda gone across the valley, circled Redrock, then come in from the opposite direction with the yarn that they were combin' the hills for me.'

'I don't think so. Ed, I believe they turned off back there at my homestead and took the road through the hills figuring that the posse would ride through to Redrock. In that case they'd come out on the other side of the mesa.'

Ed's lean jaws tightened. 'Then if we can get into the hills before they come out we can ambush the buzzards along the trail. Let's go!'

They rode to the ranch, went over it until satisfied that nobody was about, then struck for the mesa looming a couple of miles ahead of them. They found no fresh mounts at the Circle C and were forced to keep to their own jaded pair. They rode through the split between mesa and hills and headed towards the place where the hills trail debouched on the range, realizing that they were taking a desperate gamble.

They lost the race against time. With two hundred yards to go they saw a string of horsemen file from the trees and pull up abruptly at sight of the two approaching horsemen.

Recognition came almost instantly, and they heard Dave Culpepper's triumphant cry, 'It's the Kid! Boys, we got 'em nailed to the mast! *Get 'em!*'

He raised his Winchester and fired, but his bullet was aimed at Jim and the only thing that saved the boy was the sudden movement of Jim's horse as he swung him about. Ed had drawn his own rifle from the boot; now, his horse standing like a rock, he raised it and fired. But Dave's men were moving spurring towards them, fanning out and bending low in their saddles. Ed cursed as he missed and wheeled to follow Jim.

'The mesa!' Jim called over his shoulder. 'We can hold 'em, one at each trail, until Trotter gets here!'

For Dave was unaware of the dramatic climax in the courthouse that morning. He did not know that his scheme had boomeranged. He could not explain the presence of the brothers, and he didn't try to explain it. One of them was an outlaw with a price on his head; the other was aiding in his escape. Dave spurred on savagely, a tight grimace of triumph on his face.

The Circle C horses were fresher and faster; they closed the distance rapidly. Dave's men were firing steadily, although they knew that a hit from the back of a galloping horse would be a pure accident. The accident happened. Jim, speeding beside his brother, saw Ed jerk erect in the saddle, then slump over, a spasm of agony crossing his face.

He started to check his horse. 'Ed, you're hit!'

'Just—nicked. Keep goin' damn you!'

They reached the mouth of the ravine trail and turned into it, and the horses started laboring up the steep grade, grunting with the effort. Ed was sitting erect now, but his face was tight and the color of dirty chalk and he gripped the horn tightly. He halted his horse and said, 'You go on; I'll hold 'em.' He turned the horse and levered a shell into the Winchester.

Jim turned also. 'We'll both hold 'em.'

Ed cursed him. 'You ain't got a rifle. I have. Go on!'

Jim looked at him steadily for a moment, then turned as Ed raised the rifle. He heard its whiplike crack as he sent his horse lunging up the trail. Fifty yards farther he stopped and turned. The mouth of the ravine was empty except for a horse that was down and a rider who was trying to extricate himself.

Jim yelled, 'Come on, Ed! I'll cover you!'

Ed turned his horse and started up the trail, and Jim fired twice at the head of a horse which appeared around the shoulder of rock. The range was too great for a hand gun, but the horse was jerked back and once more they struggled upward.

And then Ed's horse gave out. It uttered a long, despairing gasp and its legs collapsed. It settled down slowly and Ed struggled free. And now Jim saw blood on his shirt front and realized with a sudden sinking feeling that Ed had been shot through and through.

He got off his horse and, despite Ed's savage curses, pushed his brother into the saddle. He said, 'You can use that rifle better from atop a horse.'

They climbed in short spurts, Jim dragging the weary horse after him. He kept looking back but nobody came into sight. The man who had gone down with the horse had worked clear and had joined his companions. Jim toiled on, panting and sweating with effort. Some of them he knew would go up the other trail; if he and Ed did not reach the top before them they would be hopelessly trapped. Three horsemen were following them now, but they seemed content to keep at a distance, no doubt giving their pals on the other trail time to reach the summit.

If we can make the cave, Jim thought, *we can hide and they won't be able to get at us. Trotter'll hear the shots and know where we are.*

And then his own horse quit.

Ed had been sagging lower and lower in the saddle, but he still clung to the Winchester. When the horse went down he fell out of the saddle and lay there. Jim, with a despairing backward glance, managed to get him over his shoulders. He staggered over the uneven footing, leaving the rifle behind him.

255

He reached the top. There was a red haze before his eyes and each labored breath threatened to be his last. He put Ed down and fell to the ground beside him. Ed's eyes were closed and there was bloody froth on his lips.

Jim wanted to lie there forever, but he knew he couldn't. He struggled up and knelt beside his brother. 'Ed! Wake up! It's just a little way; you can make it!'

Ed opened his eyes. They were clouded. Then suddenly the film cleared away and he said weakly, 'Where are we?'

'At the top of the trail. I know a good hiding place. Can you make it, Ed?'

Ed extended a hand and Jim got him to his feet.

'Where's—rifle?'

'I had to leave it.'

'Jus'—good. Always liked—six guns.'

He drew the Colt from its holster. Jim plucked a handful of shells from his belt and reloaded his own gun. He thrust the remaining shells into a pocket and said, 'Put your arm over my shoulder.'

He put his own arm about Ed's waist and they staggered out on the top of the mesa. A rifle cracked and the slug brushed Jim's hair. The other party had just reached the top of the trail. Jim fired two quick shots and Dave Culpepper and his two companions reined their horses behind a clump of rocks. Jim heard another shot behind him; he looked back and saw the three horsemen coming up the trail. They did not loiter now; they were closing in for the kill.

He dragged Ed to a little clump of trees. They would never reach the cave now, for to do so would mean crossing an open space where they would be subjected to the fire of Dave and the two with him. And the ones coming up the ravine would catch them on the flank. If he were alone, he might try a dash across the open. But that would mean leaving Ed.

He said as calmly as he could, 'We'll have to take on the three in the ravine, Ed.'

Ed gave a choking laugh. 'How? They got rifles; they can lay at the head of the trail and blast us to blazes. And even if we get them, how far do you think we'd get before Dave would be after us?'

He spoke slowly but clearly, but in the voice of a man already dead. He looked about him and went on, 'There's a thicker bunch of trees behind us. See if you can make 'em while I cover you.'

Jim nodded and turned. He got down on hands and knees to keep in the protection of the underbrush and started crawling towards the trees. He had gone halfway when a burst of savage firing broke out and he turned. Then he got to his feet, swearing in consternation.

Ed had left the shelter of the trees and was walking directly towards where Dave and his two men were hidden. He walked mechanically, like an automaton, raising each foot, pushing it forward and putting it down on the ground. His Colt was held at waist level but he wasn't firing it. The shots came from the clump of rocks behind which Dave and his men were hidden. Jim saw a gun appear, then a head; there would be a quick aim and a burst of fire, then head and gun would disappear. He couldn't tell what effect the shots had on Ed but he knew that all of them couldn't miss at that short range.

Straight on the automaton plodded, right foot, left foot, right foot again. He heard Dave yell, and his voice had the timbre of fear in it. 'By God, he can't keep comin' forever! Rush the devil!'

Two men emerged on one side of the rocks and Dave on the other. They were on foot and their guns started spitting the instant they came into sight. And then Ed began shooting. He stopped on braced legs and fired three deliberate shots. The first spun one of the men around; the second downed him. The third hit his companion squarely; he threw up his arms and folded like an empty gunny sack. Dave was the only one left on his feet; he hurled himself at this relentless Nemesis as though to overwhelm him by the weight of his heavy body.

Ed had been shooting from waist level; now he raised the gun, held it before him in fully extended arm. It roared and Dave's head jerked back as though he had been smitten by a sledge. Jim saw the ugly black hole in his forehead as he fell.

Ed stood for a moment, head lowered as though looking thoughtfully at the dead man; then he sank slowly to his knees and fell forward on his face.

Jim remained standing rigid and staring for the space of ten heartbeats. And then he heard a distant shot and a shouted call of '*Jimmie!*' It was Nancy's voice.

He was aware of movement on his left and jerked his head around. The three who had come up the ravine bed were sitting their horses at the edge of the mesa's top and Jim knew that they had also been staring at the drama which had been enacted before them. They could have dropped him in his tracks but Ed's deliberate sacrifice had held them. Now they had heard the signal shot and the voice and their only thought was that of flight. They wheeled their horses and sent them clattering down the ravine trail. . .

Jim was kneeling beside the Kid's body when they arrived. Tom and the Tepee crew came charging onto the mesa's top, their guns ready. They halted and gave one awed, comprehensive glance, then dropped from their horses and came swiftly to where Jim knelt. And behind them came Nancy and Limpy, held to the rear by her father's orders.

Nancy flung herself from her pony and came running, and there in front of them all she dropped to her knees and flung her arms about Jim. She cried, 'Jimmie, oh, Jimmie! You are safe after all!'

He kissed her. 'Yes; but it was Ed who saved me. Nancy, you should have seen him.' He told them gravely what Ed had done, and when he had finished Tom Payne took off his Stetson and said, 'He was a brave boy.'

Nancy put her fingers gently on the dead face that looked up at them. 'We'll bury him beside his Nesta. He would have wanted it that way.'

And presently they got up, and Sheriff Trotter came riding up the ravine trail with his posse and three prisoners, and Jim had to tell the story all over again. And then he rode to the Tepee with Nancy and Tom and Limpy and the crew and at last there was peace and contentment and satisfying knowledge that never again would the name of Lawson be despised.

★   ★   ★

Limpy and Tom washed the dishes that night, Jim and Nancy being otherwise engaged. When they had finished they lighted a lamp in the living room and wisely kept away from the gallery. After a while Tom got up and stole to the door. He opened it softly and words drifted in to them.

'But I'm sure it'll work, darling.' It was Nancy speaking. 'All we got to do is build it strong enough. I know the black'll fight; I wouldn't want him if he gave right up. But we can—'

The rest was lost as Tom closed the door. He looked at Limpy and shook his head sadly. 'Engaged to be married and talkin' about horses!'

'Yuh dad-ratted lunkhaid, they heerd yuh open the door. Everything's fixed up. Nancy done announced their engagement in public last week in Sage and the pore feller's roped, throwed and hawgtied. Which reminds me, Tom. Nancy'll be movin' over to the Lazy L right soon, which means that we'll hafta git used to my cookin'.'

Tom groaned and sank into a chair. 'That'll

be the finish of me. I'll never die of old age; I'll die of dyspepsia.'

'What're yuh grievin' about?' demanded Limpy. 'I'm the diddely-dad-burned son of a knock-kneed hipperpotamus that oughter be pitied! My stomick's weaker'n your'n and I gotta eat the danged stuff too!'

Photoset, printed and bound in Great Britain by
REDWOOD BURN LIMITED, Trowbridge, Wiltshire